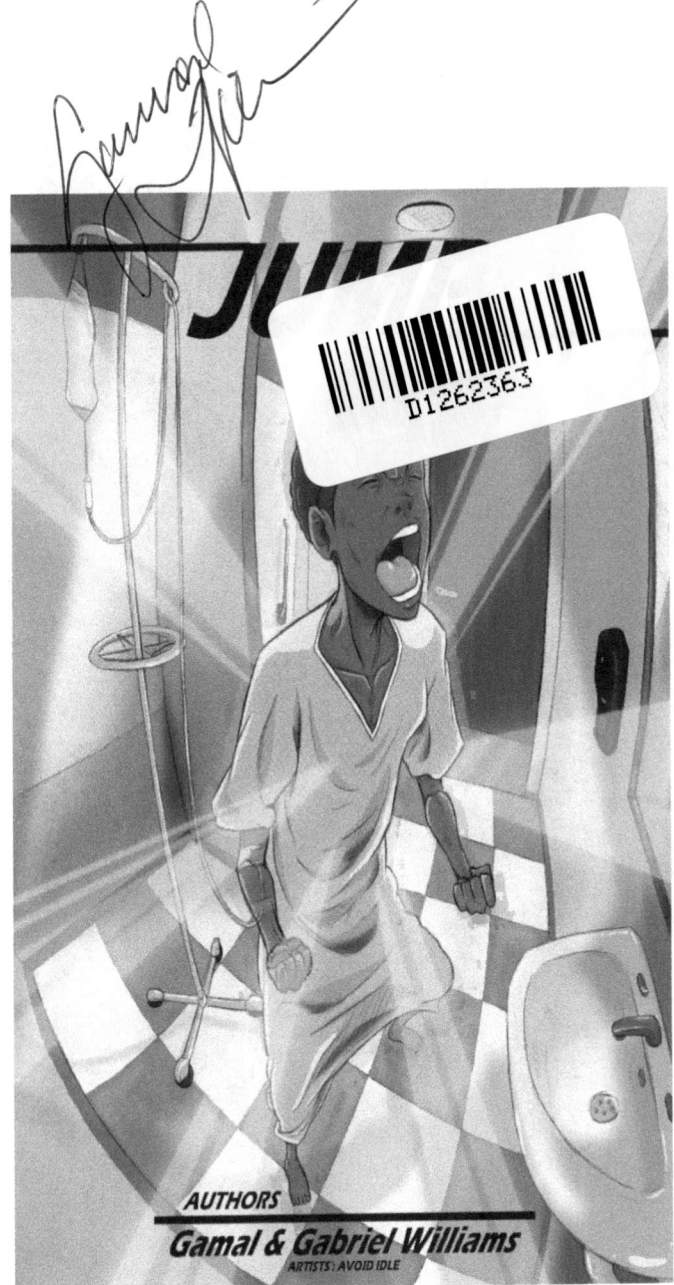

AUTHORS
Gamal & Gabriel Williams
ARTISTS: AVOID IDLE

GAMAL & GABRIEL WILLIAMS

ILLUSTRATIONS BY AVOID IDLE

Copyright © 2021 Gamal C. Williams
Jump
by Gamal C. Williams & Gabriel J. Williams
ISBN: 978-1-7355247-2-6

Printed in the United States of America
Cover and illustrations by Avoid Idle
Published by Rae Legacy Publishing

All rights reserved solely by the authors. The authors guarantee all contents are original unless cited from other noted sources and do not infringe upon the legal rights of any other person or work. The story, all names, characters, and incidents portrayed in this work are fictitious. No identification with actual persons (living or deceased), places, or buildings is intended or should be inferred.

No part of this book may be reproduced in any form without the permission of the authors. The views expressed in this book are not necessarily those of the publisher.

For

*All the little boys and girls that never get to see
themselves as heroes*

TABLE OF CONTENTS

ACKNOWLEDGEMENTS

Gabriel would like to thank:

My brothers and sisters JJ, Matthew, DeShawn, Mega, Paul, Bianca, Shari and Zari.

My Aunties Stacey, Ashley, Gina, Rose and Barb

My Uncles Anthony (Pee), Aaron, Mo, Dee and Steve.

ALLLLLLLLLLLL of my cousins!

My friends Messai, Caleb, Max, and Shawn

My teachers from Chittum Elementary, Jolliff Middle, and Changing Lives Martial Arts

Special thanks to Avoid Idle spending lots of your time on our drawings, KiLaMDaPro for letting us use your song, and Ms. Sasha for always making me feel special and encouraging me to be a writer.

And a BIG, EXTRA special thanks to Momma and David, Daddy and Kirby, Great Grandma, Nana, Nanny, Aunt Sunflower, Memaw and PopPop!

THANK YOU FOR ALL OF YOUR SUPPORT!

THERE AIN'T NO FAMILY OR FRIENDS BETTER THAN Y'ALL!!

XOXOXOXO

Gamal would like to thank:

Avoid Idle for making our vision come alive with your illustrations. You two are amazing! Thank you!

Rae Legacy Publishing for being super supportive and believing in not just me, but Gabriel. Thanks for everything.

All of my family, friends, and former shipmates that have supported every project I have done.

Ani and Livy for being my original test audience. You two beautiful young ladies are a treasure. Thank you!! 😊

And finally, to my inspiration for this project, my buddy, my son and my co-author, Gabriel.

Poppa,

When I look at you, I see a world of possibilities. The future is yours, son and there is nothing you can't accomplish. There are two things I am grateful for: knowing I will get to be there whenever you need me, and that I have been blessed that I get to watch your journey.

I love you. Forever and always.

Daddy

CHAPTER 1
ON YOUR MARK

"Let's go, Brooklyn!"

Franklin stared up into the stands, his hand up to shield his eyes from the glare of the Friday afternoon sun. He recognized the voice; it was Mom as she clapped and screamed at the top of her lungs. He had just finished his 400 meter dash and placed third in the Regional Finals. He previously beat the two boys that placed first and second earlier in the season, but that didn't matter any longer. In his biggest moment, he choked in front of the whole city. Now, his sister Brooklyn was up. She was a ruthless competitor and never missed an opportunity to remind him of her athletic superiority, as if her winning at everything wasn't enough.

Franklin and Brooklyn always tried to one-up each other, and Franklin hated losing to her. Whether it was cards, hoops, report cards, video games, even down to who could eat the fastest, he usually finished second. When Franklin received a grade on a test or in a class, Brooklyn made it her business to let him know if she received a higher one when she took the class the year prior.

When Franklin joined the school baseball team, Brooklyn responded and joined the tennis team, then was elected team captain. When Brooklyn won her first tennis match, she paraded around the house for days, and gave a blow-by-blow account of how her moment of glory unfolded. She did it only because she knew it got under his skin, as his first game wasn't until the following week.

The one sport where she truly outshone him though, was track. Franklin was good; Brooklyn was other-worldly good!

As he sat in the center infield, Franklin studied Brooklyn as she stood behind the starter block. He watched with envious eyes as she went through her pre-race routine of stretches, practiced getting out of the starting block, then jogged around as she shook her arms and legs to keep them loose. The crowd of onlookers, many there to support their high school, all cheered and called her name as the race's start drew near. They never called his name, however. The announcer began to announce the participants over the stadium's public address system.

"In Lane Two, from Eastwood High School, Taylor McGovern."

He looked around at his fellow teammates, many of them on their feet in excitement. Brooklyn was ranked number one in the city in the 100 and 400 meter dash, 400 meter hurdles, and was the anchor on the 400 and 1600 meter relay squads. Franklin was ranked second overall coming into today, but after his poor showing, his ranking would drop.

"In Lane Three, from Parkview High School, Latisha Collins."

The smattering of applause rose and died quickly in anticipation of Brooklyn's name being called. A reporter from the Norfolk Chronicle approached him earlier that season after he had just won the 400 meter dash. He had just smashed the old boy's school record, yet the first question the reporter asked instantly reminded him of his place in the Williams family athletic hierarchy.

2

"Franklin, congratulations on your race today. How does it feel to know you are only three district records away from tying your sister?"

In his moment of glory, Brooklyn somehow was given the spotlight. Franklin sat in the infield, yet his spirit felt cold. He was bathed in sunlight, but always in Brooklyn's shadow. He knew deep down that she was the better athlete. At just about every practice, she would beat everyone on the field, boy or girl. On that Friday afternoon, all of Norfolk was about to see what they came for; the fastest athlete in the city put on a show. Even the announcer sounded excited.

"In Lane Four, from Western High School, Brooklyn Williams!"

The crowd went wild. He didn't clap though. He simply sat there, his legs stretched out in front of him as he leaned back with both arms extended and his hands on the ground. While many observers could mistake his lack of enthusiasm for outright jealousy, that was only partially true. He was a little jealous of her popularity, but in truth, he just wanted to go home. He decided to focus on the next day, let his mind drift off to Mom and Dad's company picnic. He would get to see Danielle again. In the stands, Mom, Dad, and his Uncle Jason saw him brooding in the center of the field.

"He is taking it harder than I thought," Mom stated disappointedly.

Uncle Jason dismissively waved his hand towards the field.

"He'll be fine. He had a bad day. Happens to the best of them."

Uncle Jason was always nonchalant about things like this. A former athlete himself, he still held multiple boys track and field, football, and wrestling records at Eastwood High. Mom, who was two years older than her baby brother and had never liked his blasé attitude, rolled her eyes at his comment, then turned to Dad.

"He isn't even excited for Brooklyn's race?"

Dad gently patted her leg.

"I'll talk to him, honey."

The race participants were in their lanes, gave themselves last minute pep talks, and received final instructions from coaches or encouragement from teammates, all except for Brooklyn. She was already in a crouched position, one foot pressed against the starting block, the other in front of her. Her head was down. Franklin spotted her laser focus. Brooklyn was in her zone. *How does she do that? No fear. Never worrying about what people say or think. I wish I could block everything out like that.*

"Athletes, take your mark!"

Brooklyn placed her other foot back and rested it into the block as the rest of the racers assumed their positions. They all glanced down at her as they readied themselves, they tried not to show their trepidation, but Franklin could see by the looks in their eyes, Brooklyn's demeanor had intimidated them. *Dang! They already lost!*

"Get set!"

When Brooklyn raised her head, he could see her eyes. The intensity, the focus, the determination was inspiring. More than her athletic ability, it was her will to win, her drive to be the best that he envied most. The sun beamed down on the track and gave a slight glimmer to her pecan-complected skin bathed in cocoa butter. Her thick hair was tied into two French braids that ended at the base of her neck.

Suddenly, a gust of wind blew, left to right. Franklin watched the ripple it caused in the grass infield and assessed the first part of the race would be into the wind. His eyes then focused back on Brooklyn. She squinted her left eye hard. The wind had blown something into it. Franklin grew anxious and mumbled under his breath.

"Stand up, Brook! Take the false start!"

BANG!

It was too late. The seven other girls in the race took off much faster than Brooklyn. The debris in her eye had thrown her off her game. As the race progressed, moving from his right to his left, the girl from Eastwood High held a sizable lead. Franklin shook his head. *This doesn't look good.* Calls of encouragement for Brooklyn rained down from the stands while family and friends from the opposing schools all cheered their student-athletes on.

"Your sister gonna lose, Frank," his teammate Carlos chided.

I should be so lucky! He watched her struggle as she entered turn one. *Brook could win this race with one leg! One eye closed isn't going to stop her.* As the race progressed around the curved part of the track, and headed into turn number two, he rolled over onto his stomach to watch as the race moved behind him. Mom and Dad grew nervous of Brooklyn's poor start.

"Come on, baby! You got this, Brooklyn Rae!"

"Push, Brooklyn! PUSH!"

Uncle Jason seemed unfazed...and unimpressed.

"I won a race with a pulled hamstring, once. Remember, Sis?"

Mom hated when he bragged, and this was not the time for his inflated ego.

"No one cares, Jason!"

Brooklyn's eye hurt badly. She couldn't break her stride to rub it, nor could she open it and let the wind produce tears. She clamped it shut and pushed on. She was a good five meters behind the girl from Eastwood and was in fifth place.

Straightaways were the strength of any runner, and Brooklyn was the best at them. When she reached her full stride, Brooklyn ran with a grace and beauty that was effortless. While others seemed to be running, Franklin thought Brooklyn danced, her long-legged strides comparable to a ballerina that gracefully sailed across the stage.

Something is not right! Brooklyn didn't pick up speed like normal. He waited on her to close the gap, but it never happened. His doubting teammate Carlos saw it too.

"Telling you, Franklin. Brook is about to go down!"

Franklin jumped up, pushed Carlos to the side, and ran for turn three. He couldn't stand when Brooklyn received all of the accolades, and it put a knot in his stomach when she rubbed it into his face, but he really despised when someone doubted either of them. In this moment, it was them against the world. He ran towards her and shouted at the top of his lungs.

"LET'S GO, BROOK! PUSH THROUGH IT! YOU GOT THIS!"

Brooklyn was the overwhelming favorite yet brought up the rear of the race. She kept her stride, as she fought through the pain. The race passed through turn three and entered turn four, the girl from Eastwood ten meters ahead of her. The crowd screamed louder than ever. The small Eastwood cheering section was the loudest. Suddenly, Franklin heard something he had never heard before. Something he thought he always wanted to hear, but the sound of it broke his heart. Brooklyn cried out in defeat.

"UHHHHHHH!"

He ran alongside of her in the grass, willing her into turn four.

"NO, BROOK! DON'T QUIT! GET 'EM ON THE NEXT TURN!"

"WILLIAMS!" screamed their coach. "GET OVER HERE!"

Franklin ignored his coach. Brooklyn never acknowledged Franklin's presence, but she had to know she wasn't alone. She had to know he was right there with her. He knew she heard him because then, it happened.

"AAAAAARRRRRRGGGGGHHHHH!!!!!"

Brooklyn let out a scream that terrified everyone at the field that day. Mom and Dad thought she had pulled a hamstring or rolled her ankle. Franklin thought something was wrong too, until he saw what she did next. That scream wasn't pain, it was fury, it was strength, it was beautiful.

Somewhere, somewhere deep within her, Brooklyn found a gear Franklin didn't know she had. She accelerated like she had wings. The wind meant nothing. Friction and gravity no longer existed. She moved like she was weightless. As the gap between her and first place closed from ten meters, down to eight meters, then down to five meters in a matter of moments, the crowd all stood to their feet.

The Western High School track team, both boys and girls, all leapt from their seats and screamed in excitement as Brooklyn blew past all of her competitors except one. The girl from Eastwood tried to kick it into high gear, a desperate attempt to cling to her ever-decreasing lead, but the force of nature behind her that was Brooklyn Williams, would not be denied.

Franklin anxiously watched from behind as Brooklyn and the other girl leaned across the finish line. It wasn't until he saw all of their teammates run onto the track, all with huge smiles on their faces as they cheered and jumped, that he realized Brooklyn had won. He smiled bigger than he ever had before. He couldn't be any happier for her than if he had won his own race. For this, he would gladly take all the ribbing she was sure to give him.

Franklin ran to join her and their teammates as they celebrated. He glanced up into the stands to see Mom and Dad. They too were elated as they jumped up and down. They paused in their celebration to smile at him, happy he put his own brooding aside to be there for his sister. Uncle Jason pounded his chest!

"That's MY niece! That's MY NIECE!"

Franklin smiled, then went to find Brooklyn. As he waded through the sea of people on the track, he spotted Carlos standing next to Brooklyn smiling, as she leaned

9

into their coach. She was exhausted, her eye was bloodshot, and she was drenched in sweat.

"Told you she had that thing, Frank!"

When Brooklyn spotted Franklin, she scowled. Her exhausted smile turned into a frown. The hurt in her voice was broken only by her deep gasps for oxygen.

"You......*gasp*......you *doubted me?*"

"*NO! I was the one cheering you on! I was right there with...*"

"Yeah? When? I saw you...*gasp*...sitting there when I...*gasp*...made turn two!"

The venom in her voice pierced his ears. *How could she not know it was me?*

"I'm telling you, Brook. I was the one running with you at turn three!"

His plea fell on deaf ears. She walked off under the help of their coach. He was motionless, despondent by her unwillingness to believe him. He walked back to the infield and grabbed his jacket. Brooklyn rolled her eyes at him in turn. He stormed off the infield, across the track, and through the gate that led to the parking lot. Though Mom and Dad couldn't hear Brooklyn and Franklin's exchange over the excitement of the crowd, they could see by Franklin's reaction something was wrong.

"What happened? Where is he going, Brian?"

"I don't know, honey. I'll find out."
"HA! Yeah, that's your kid alright, Sis. You were a sore loser when I used to beat you too!"

Dad glared at Uncle Jason. Uncle Jason's smile disappeared. Mom pushed Uncle Jason in anger. Dad turned towards the end of the bleacher aisle. He struggled to navigate through the people still shouting or attempting to exit. Slowed down by the crowd, Franklin's pace towards the parking lot was much faster than Dad's pace to exit the bleachers. From his vantage point, Dad could see the anger and hurt on Franklin's face. *I need to stop him; talk to him.* He made it to the end of the bleachers and leaned over the rail just as Franklin entered the parking lot.

"Franklin!"

Franklin dejectedly glanced up at his father and shook his head.

"Where are you going, Franklin?"

Franklin didn't respond. He ran away hard and fast. Dad watched with disappointment as Franklin darted in between parked cars towards the main road. Franklin's eyes filled with tears. The hurt and rage he felt towards Brooklyn grew with each step of his sneakers as they pounded on the pavement. He couldn't stand to be around Brooklyn or his family.

They always root harder for her than me! I tried to be supportive, and she still treated me like her enemy! All Mom and Dad do is tell us that we can't always try and beat each other, but she doesn't listen. They are gonna make her apologize, but she won't mean it. Next chance she gets, she is gonna embarrass me.

He wished there was something he could beat her at, something he could rub in her face. Something that hurt, something she wanted more than anything so he could take it from her. His frustration and anger grew as he realized she bested him at everything. He ran faster while tears streamed down his face. His breaths were hard and heavy. He let out a painful scream like the one Brooklyn did moments earlier, but where she found the will to go on, Franklin stopped.

He was on the main boulevard, out of breath and openly crying. The emotion of the day had defeated him. He had lost twice that afternoon, once on the track, the other in his heart. The sun had begun to fade away and darkness grew. The headlights of cars on the busy road made him turn from their view. The roar of their engines drowned out his sobs. He found himself spinning around, as he thought about what he should do next. He paused, took a deep breath to collect himself, then began to walk down the sidewalk. He decided to go home.

Back at the field, the final meets were now complete. After her iconic triumph in the 400 meter dash, Brooklyn gathered herself, and full of adrenaline, she went out and anchored the 1600 meter relay, and set the new regional school record. When her final race was over, she ran into the bleachers to find her parents and uncle.

"Mom! Did you see me out..."

"Brooklyn, what did you say to your brother?"

"That traitor!"

"*Excuse me*, young lady?"

"Mom, he was rooting against me!"

"No, he wasn't. Brook, your brother was right there beside you."
"Carlos said..."

"Carlos is a liar!" Mom snapped. "Whatever he said, he lied! Your brother jumped up and ran alongside of you."

Brooklyn was stunned and ashamed. "That was him?"

Dad was upset in her lack of trust in Franklin.

"Who else would it have been, Brooklyn? Whatever happened, you need to make it right with him. I have never seen him so happy when you won."

"Mannnn...I'm so sorry, Mom. Dad. Where is he?"

"He ran off. Figured he was heading home. We'll see him at the house."

Uncle Jason waved his hand at Mom and Dad.

"Don't listen to that! Revel in this moment. You ran one helluva race, Brook!"

Mom had finally had enough.

"Shut up, Jason! I won't allow you to do to them what you tried to do to us! Franklin and Brooklyn are brother and sister! Not enemies, not rivals, brother and sister! They should be supporting each other, trusting in each other!"

Mom turned her fury towards Brooklyn.

"Brooklyn, you are so quick to want to be better than Franklin, to beat him, you never stopped to see that in his lowest moment, he put all of it aside to be there for you! This stops NOW! RIGHT NOW! Or I'll see to it that you never participate in another sport again. If winning

13

at all costs, costs you the ones that love you, was the price worth it?"

Brooklyn slumped her shoulders and lowered her head and eyes to the ground. She heard the voice that screamed and cheered her on. *How did I not know that was him?* The shame that she didn't recognize it was Franklin that cheered her on, wiped all the joy from her come from behind victory away. She knew she had to apologize, but apologies weren't something she was good at or liked to do. She loved him and never wanted to hurt him. She was hard on him, yes, but that didn't mean she enjoyed inflicting pain upon him.

"Let me say goodbye to the team. I'll meet you at the car."

She dejectedly walked back to the infield where her teammates were gathered. She collected her track suit and bag, said her goodbyes, then jogged over to meet her parents. Uncle Jason had already departed on his motorcycle. During the ride home, Brooklyn searched the sidewalks, side streets, and parking lot of every strip mall, convenience store and gas station she saw. Unable to locate him, she started to text him repeatedly.

> *Brooklyn: Bro, WRU?*
> *Brooklyn: Come on, Franklin. Mom and Dad*
> *told me what u did.*
> *Brooklyn: Carlos is a liar! I should have known it*
> *was u!*
> *Brooklyn: Franklin????*
> *Brooklyn: ?????????*

He never answered.

"He isn't answering any of my texts."
Dad glanced at her reflection in the rearview mirror.

"Give him some time, baby girl. He needs space to clear his head."

Brooklyn slid down in her seat; guilt ridden from what she had done. When the family car pulled into the driveway of their house, Brooklyn hopped out before Dad could put the car into park, let alone turn the engine off. She darted for the front door, entered her code, then disarmed the security system. She raced upstairs to see if Franklin was in his room. She swung his door open and saw he was asleep. Disappointed in herself, her mouth turned up.

"Sorry."

She gently closed the door and went to her room.

CHAPTER 2
BREAK, FAST

Franklin awoke the next morning, still angered from the night before. He laid flat on his back. His eyes burned as they adjusted to the sunlight that filled his room. He hadn't even removed his track suit the night before. When he arrived home, he merely dropped his bag and laid across his bed. Franklin saw all of Brooklyn's texts, but had no desire to talk to her.

When Mom, Dad, and Brooklyn arrived at the house, he quickly dove under the covers, turned his face towards the wall, and feigned being asleep. It took everything he had not to jump up and yell at Brooklyn when she entered his room. *You're sorry?! You believed Carlos over me??? CARLOS?!?!?* But he didn't. He simply laid in bed, the blanket over his head, bit his bottom lip, and stared at the wall.

The clinging sounds of pots and pans, silverware drawers as they opened and closed, and the pop of hot grease on the stove meant one of his parents was preparing breakfast. As he stared at the ceiling, he had one thought: *Please let Dad cook breakfast today.* He pulled himself out of the bed and slowly walked over to the bathroom that connected his and Brooklyn's room. He leaned into the door and listened for any sound. *Silence. She must still be sleeping.*

Franklin entered the bathroom and immediately locked the door that led to Brooklyn's room. His track suit stuck to his body, sticky from sweat. He peeled his clothes off and climbed into the shower. After his shower, he toweled off then went back into his room. He stood in front of his closet and stared at his clothes. It was an important day. After breakfast, the family would leave for Mom and Dad's company picnic. The company picnic meant he would get to see Danielle again. *God, if you're listening...please don't let me embarrass myself with Danielle! Please!* The thought repeated over and over in Franklin's mind. He still felt the sting from yesterday's events. Though he tried his best to focus, he couldn't.

"Breakfast!" shouted Mom.

"Okay, Mom!" cried Brooklyn from her room.

Franklin shook his head. *Dang! Mom cooked! I hope it isn't nasty!* The food smelled different than the usual bacon and eggs she used to make on Saturday mornings. *Please don't be that turkey bacon and egg substitute again.* He turned his nose up at the thought. Last time Mom went on a health binge, everyone in the house had to come along for the ride. Two nights ago, it was vegetarian lasagna, but instead of lasagna noodles, she thinly sliced zucchini into ribbons, and substituted them for good, old-fashioned pasta. Dad smiled as he ate his. Franklin and Brooklyn did not. They thought it tasted like dirt, "earthy" was the way Brooklyn described it. He took another sniff of the air. *Whatever she is cooking, stinks!*

Franklin finished getting dressed. He slid his sneakers on, then examined himself in the full-length mirror that hung on his closet door. *Think I'll go with the boots instead.* He switched from his sneakers into his boots and took a quick peek at himself. *Oh, yeah! I look good!* He wore a red t-shirt, blue jeans, and black boots. He smiled at his full ensemble. He had to make sure his outfit was perfect. His confidence took a slight hit as nervousness washed over him again.

18

Though extremely handsome, Franklin was just as shy. He stood five-feet, nine-inches tall, with a thick, four-inch afro he wanted to eventually twist into dreadlocks. His adolescent body was thin, but well defined, mostly due to his participation in team sports. Franklin walked over to the dresser and began to pick and sculpt his afro. Satisfied with his hair, he set the pick down on the dresser and stared at himself in the mirror.

Okay, Franklin. This time you ARE gonna talk to her! You aren't gonna be nervous. You are gonna walk right up to her and say...

He turned his head away from the mirror, slightly squinted his eyes, raised one eyebrow, and smiled smoothly before turning back to the mirror.

"Hey, Danielle. Glad to see you made it to this little party."

"Hiiiiiii, Franklin," he said in a poor mockery of Danielle's voice. Then he switched back to his own smooth, buttery voice.

"So, Danielle. I have always wanted to ask you..."

"Oh, Franklin!"

That response wasn't him. He turned around in horror and embarrassment to see Brooklyn at the threshold of the bathroom. Franklin dropped his head. *She is NEVER gonna let me live this down.*

"Yes! YES! I'll be your girlfriend!"

She ran up to him and threw her arms around him. He pushed her off.

"Shut up!"

20

She let out a hearty laugh and shoved her baby brother in the chest. There was an uneasy tension in the air. Brooklyn heard anger in Franklin's voice and understood why. Her joy from teasing him faded away. Franklin surmised that shove was as close as he would get to an apology from her, but it wasn't enough. Yesterday hurt and he wasn't going to just let it go. Brooklyn tried anyway.

"You look good, Frankie. Dena..."

"Danielle."

"Well, excuse me. *Danielle* would be a fool not to like you. Who is this Danielle anyway?"

He didn't want to answer her. The last thing he wanted was to give her more ammo to attack him with later, and after yesterday, he wasn't going to let her off the hook so easily. Brooklyn knew she should apologize, and genuinely wanted to, but she viewed an admission of guilt or wrongdoing as a failure, and she hated to fail. She decided to just get it over with.

"Soooooo...about yesterday..."

Franklin turned away from her.

"Forget about it."

She reached out and gently grasped his upper arm.

"No, Frankie. I was wrong. I shouldn't have doubted you."

Franklin pulled away from her grasp. He didn't want to look at her.

"Yeah, you were."

His anger got the best of him. His brow scrunched as he spun around.

"How could you ever think I would go against you?"

She dropped her head and began to rock side to side.

"I know...I got caught up in the moment. Then when I didn't see you at the finish line, I thought you were still mad about your race."

"Doesn't matter. I'm never going to root against you, even though you get on my nerves when you win."

Brooklyn noticed the slight, wry smile on his face. Never one to display her emotions like a normal fifteen-year-old girl, Brooklyn reverted to her bullying tactics, and punched him in the arm.

"OWWW! Really?"

"Brooklyn! Franklin! Breakfast! We are having turkey bacon and vegetarian eggs!" shouted Mom from the kitchen.

Franklin and Brooklyn stuck their tongues out in disgust, feigned placing their fingers in their mouth as if they needed to vomit, then they both laughed out loud. Even though he was still mad at her, their shared mutual feelings towards their common enemy of Mom's vegetarian meals won him over.

"Kids!" hollered Dad full of frustration. "Get down here and eat this food your Mama cooked!"

"Think he just doesn't wanna suffer alone?" asked Franklin.

"Misery loves company, I guess. Come on, lover boy. Let's go get vegetarian eggs!"

They made their way into the hallway and headed towards the stairs. Things between the siblings went back to normal without a moment's hesitation. A simple walk down the hallway, down the stairs and into the kitchen became a competition. Brooklyn shoved Franklin and gave a slight grin. He knew this meant the race was on!

Brooklyn pushed him into the wall lined with photos of both of their past athletic triumphs and darted towards the top of the stairs. He reached for her upper arm to pull her back. The sounds of their feet as they ran down the stairs and loud bumps when their torsos hit the walls echoed throughout the house. Brooklyn leapt off the stairs and landed with a thud, a split second before Franklin reached the bottom. She turned and smiled at Franklin.

"Too slow!"

Mom shook her head disapprovingly.

"Now, are we gonna start this day with you two locked in mortal combat?"

Mom held a skillet in her hand as she hovered over the breakfast table and scooped large amounts of vegetarian eggs onto everyone's plates. Dad was already seated, his eyes wide as he saw the large helping of unwanted eggs placed on his plate. He dreadfully gazed at Franklin and Brooklyn.

JUMP
BREAK, FAST

"Come on, kids. Your Mama cooked us a healthy, *delicious* breakfast."

They both scrunched their faces, knowing they all had to suffer through it, as they begrudgingly sat down to the table. Mom didn't appreciate the sarcasm in Dad's tone. Franklin plopped down in his seat.

"Mom, why do we have to eat this?"

"Yeah, Mom," echoed Brooklyn. "You are the healthiest, fittest person we know. We can have some real food from time to time."

"Well, we can always be healthier. Besides, we have two future Olympians at the table. Got to fuel your bodies correctly. Isn't that right, Honey?"

Dad just stared at his plate as if his mound of eggs and turkey bacon mocked him. Mom began to dig into her breakfast.

"Isn't that right...Honey?"

Dad winced then peeked at Franklin and Brooklyn.

"Oh, yes! Great fuel for the..."

"HEY, FAMILY!"

Uncle Jason burst through the back door, next to the refrigerator that led to the backyard. As usual, his arrival was welcomed by Franklin, Brooklyn, and Mom. Dad shook his head and returned to labor through breakfast. Uncle Jason scanned everyone's plate and scrunched his nose in disgust.

"What. Is. THAT?!?!"

"It's healthy, Jason," Mom remarked dismissively.

Uncle Jason turned his gaze to Franklin and Brooklyn.

"She gave you that 'future Olympians' line, didn't she?"

Franklin and Brooklyn giggled. Even Dad raised his eyebrows in agreement. Mom was not amused.
"Jason, what do you want?"

"Dang, Sis. I can't even drop by and see the family? Besides, looks like I am saving these kids from malnutrition!"

"Jason, we are not having this discussion again."

Uncle Jason waved her off, pulled out a chair next to Mom and sat down. He grabbed a piece of turkey bacon and took a bite, then promptly spit it out into a napkin.

"Lord, woman! What are you doing to these kids?"

Franklin and Brooklyn chuckled, then quickly quieted down when they saw the look on Mom's face. They averted their eyes from Mom and Uncle Jason and onto their plates.

"I don't blame you, honestly," commented Uncle Jason. "I remember when we were kids, your mom started drinking some wheat grass, barley root, pinecone breakfast mess."

"It was a high-protein whey shake," snapped Mom.

"It was a glass full of grass and dirt," quipped Uncle Jason. "And it didn't help her! She could never beat me!"

Uncle Jason burst out into laughter, but Dad became annoyed. Much like Franklin was with Brooklyn, Dad didn't take too kindly to anyone doubting or mocking Mom, no matter how much Dad hated the breakfast she made.

"Well, I am enjoying this. I feel healthier already!"

Dad winked as his eyes met Mom's. Mom blushed. Franklin and Brooklyn's eyes grew wider, and their heads snapped in Dad's direction. Franklin skeptically shook his head. *He must reeeaaaalllly love Mom because this is nasty!* Mom returned Dad's smile, appreciative that he took her side no matter how much he despised the food, then turned back to Franklin and Brooklyn.

"Eat up! We have a busy day and a long drive to the cookout."

They both slowly reached for their forks, neither wanted to be the first one to sample Mom's latest concoction. Dad shoveled the contents of his plate into his mouth. Franklin and Brooklyn gaped at Dad, amazed by how fast he ate. Dad snuck a peek in their direction and raised his eyebrows, a gesture for them to start eating, and to just eat it fast. They looked at each other once more and accepted their fate.

From the first bite, Franklin knew he made a mistake. *BLECK! These things she calls eggs taste like cardboard!* Brooklyn was in full competition mode, and stuffed her food into her mouth so fast, Franklin thought she might not just beat him, but Dad as well. Franklin was perfectly fine with Brooklyn completing breakfast first, however. Mom became visibly upset.

"Brooklyn Rae Williams! Is that how a lady eats? Act like you have some home training and conduct yourself appropriately at my table."

"Yes, Ma'am," she mumbled through her fully stuffed mouth that made her cheeks bulge like a chipmunk.

Franklin snickered and Mom turned all her attention his way.

"You too, Mr. Williams. Eat up! Big day today. Don't want to be late for Danielle, now do we?"

"That *is* right," proclaimed Uncle Jason. "You get to see your little girlfriend today. You excited?"

"Oh, he is excited alright!" teased Brooklyn. "He was in the mirror practicing his lines and everything. Ain't that right, Mack Daddy?!"

Everyone at the table smiled, everyone except Franklin. Franklin instantly regretted that he told anyone about Danielle. He stopped chewing, slumped his shoulders and dropped his chin to his chest. *Why did I ever tell any of them about Danielle? And why does she look for every opportunity to embarrass me? I'd say this is "Pick on Franklin Day," but that's every, single day around here. I can't stand this family!*

"Leave your brother alone, Brook. Nothing wrong with a little puppy love," expressed Dad. Dad wanted to make Franklin feel more comfortable. It had the complete opposite effect. Brooklyn reached for his cheeks to pinch him.

27

"Awwwwwwwww. Are you a cute, little, love-sick puppy?"

Brooklyn could be relentless when she wanted to be. Franklin had had enough.

"Can I be excused?"

"Not until you have finished that food," scolded Mom. Brooklyn ended her teasing, and a confused look grew on her face.

"Seriously though, why don't I remember this girl?"

"Maybe because last year you were lip-locked with Caleb all day," Franklin replied.

Brooklyn froze, her vegetarian egg filled fork suspended in air. She darted her eyes angrily at Franklin then nervously at Mom and Dad. Dad avoided making eye contact with her. The thought of his baby girl kissing a boy made him squirm in his seat. Mom sat back in her chair, surprised by this revelation. Franklin suddenly had a newfound interest in cleaning his plate. He scarfed his food down, most of it stuffed in his cheeks, then dropped his fork on his plate.

CLING!

"Now **gulp**may **gulp**I be excused?"

Mom and Dad shook their heads and laughed.

"Go on, boy. Be ready to leave in twenty minutes."

Franklin rose from the table, collected his plate, and headed for the sink. He paused as he passed

Brooklyn who was still seated at the table. He had to take a moment to gloat, a moment he couldn't pass up. He bent over and whispered in her ear.

"Too slow."

Brooklyn frowned then rushed to finish her food.

"Well," began Uncle Jason, "that is my cue to leave."

"So soon?" quipped Dad.

Uncle Jason rose from the table, then leaned over and kissed Mom on the crown of her head.

"Later, Sis."

"Where are you heading off to?" Mom inquired.

"To the Pancake House to get some *real* food. Y'all have fun. Later kids."

Franklin didn't respond to Uncle Jason, instead he ran back upstairs. He walked into his room and closed the door. He sat down on his bed and sulked. His emotions ranged from anger at Brooklyn, to embarrassment during breakfast. His mind was all over the place and unable to focus on anything. He simply stared at the floor, lost in his thoughts. Precisely twenty minutes later, Dad called out from the bottom of the stairs.

"Everyone ready?"

Brooklyn was in the bathroom, ensuring her hair was perfect. When she heard Dad's voice she rolled her eyes.

"Coming! " she cried out.

Better go get Frankie. She opened the door that led to his room and saw Franklin sat on the edge of the bed.

"Let's go, baby bro!"

He didn't respond.

"Franklin!"

Franklin jumped and lifted his head up, his eyes wide from fright. Brooklyn frowned curiously.

"You okay?"

"Yeah, I'm good."

"Well, it's time to go."

"Okay. I'm coming."

Franklin followed Brooklyn out of his room, down the hallway and downstairs. Mom and Dad had changed into polo shirts bearing Dad's company logo over the left breast. Mom smiled when she saw them.

"You two look amazing."

Brooklyn turned her mouth up and scanned Franklin's clothes.

"Mom don't lie to this boy. He looks like a toddler. Did Mom pick that outfit out for you, little boy?"

He quickly scanned his outfit. *What's wrong with what I'm wearing? Does it look that bad?* He turned his

30

attention to Brooklyn and the mischievous grin on her face only angered him.

"Shut up and get in the car!"

"Franklin! Since when do we tell people to shut up?"

"Sorry, Mom," he replied the scowled at Brooklyn. "Please be quiet and get in the car."

Dad decided to diffuse the situation as he exited through the front door.

"Sounds good to me!"

Mom turned and walked outside as well, with Brooklyn right behind, but not before she popped him in the back of the head as she passed him. Mom's motherly intuition must have gone off. Though she didn't see Brooklyn hit him, she knew something had happened.

"Brooklyn......."

The family piled into the car, Dad started the engine, and off they went on the forty-five-minute trek up to the park where for the cookout. Franklin and Brooklyn braced themselves for Mom and Dad to discuss yesterday's events. When neither Mom nor Dad brought it up during breakfast, they both realized the conversation would happen in the car. Dad looked at the two of them through the rearview mirror.

"Kids. We need to talk about yesterday."

Mom turned around in her seat to address them both.

31

"You two have got to stop this constant need to beat the other. You're starting to not trust each other, and I don't like it."

"Now, we are not saying there is anything wrong with a little competition..." explained Dad.

Mom's head snapped towards Dad. He could see the scowl on her face from the corner of his eye but finished his sentence all the same.

"...but what we are saying is it should never mean you beat each other at all costs, or you let it develop into what happened yesterday."

Mom rolled her eyes at Dad and returned to Franklin and Brooklyn.

"Brooklyn, your brother loves you. Yesterday, at that race, I have never seen him so scared that you might lose."

Franklin noticed Brooklyn's left knee bounced as she stared out of the window with her arms folded. She was angry, but even more embarrassed. Mom and Dad didn't know Franklin and Brooklyn had already talked. Franklin decided to save her.

"Mom, Brook and I are good. We talked this morning."

Brooklyn was surprised Franklin spoke up for her. She turned her gaze to him as he talked to Mom, who appeared satisfied with this new information, but only barely. Mom pursed her lips and gave a scolding glare at them both, then turned around in her seat.

"Good. I never want to see that from you two again. Understood?"

"Yes, Ma'am," the two responded in chorus.

Grateful the uncomfortable exchange was over, Brooklyn placed her ear pods in her ears and began to listen to music. Dad reached for the car stereo and tuned to sports talk radio, his usual whenever he drove. Mom reached into her purse, pulled out her tablet, and began to read a book.

Franklin noticed they were about to get on the highway and felt a knot form in his stomach. *We are gonna be there soon.* He let out a long, anxious sigh then unlocked his cellphone and found Danielle's InstaBook page. Franklin often thought of sending her a friend request, but even that scared him. He didn't want her to reject him. Once again, Mom's intuition must have gone haywire. She paused in her reading and turned around to look at Franklin, who sat behind Dad.

"Relax, baby. I'm sure Danielle is a nice girl. She would be a fool not to like you."

Mom always had a way of making him feel better. He smiled at her, and hoped her proclamation was correct. Dad peaked at him through the rearview mirror as they approached a stoplight. As he eased into the breaks, he began to speak.

"It's okay to be nervous, Franklin. Just relax and be yourself, son."

Franklin nodded as his father spoke. It was easy for them to say but calming himself down was something he was never good at. He decided to ask his father a question, one that he knew Brooklyn wouldn't hear. Brooklyn bopped her head and silently mouthed the words of the song in her ears. Confident Brooklyn couldn't hear them, Franklin started his inquiry as Dad began to pull off.

"Dad, did you ever have a crush on a girl before?"

"Of course."

"Were you scared to talk to her? Scared you were going to make a fool of yourself?"

Dad laughed. He applied the car's brakes as they reached another red light then lovingly fixed his gaze on Mom.

"Oh yeah! I remember when I first saw her in biology class. She had one of the lenses in her thick glasses pressed up against a microscope, her nose scrunched up. She was studying bacteria growing in a petri dish. Her jeans were riding up on her waist and her t-shirt read *'YOU MATTER...UNLESS YOU MULTIPLY YOURSELF BY THE SPEED OF LIGHT SQUARED....THEN YOU'RE ENERGY*.'"

He chuckled. "I was hooked right there in that moment!"

"So, she was a nerd."

Mom set her tablet down and turned to him.

"What's wrong with nerds, Franklin?"

"Nothing, I guess. So, what did you do after you saw her, Dad?"

"He walked up to me and told me a corny bacteria joke! Why are bacteria bad at math?"

Dad smiled and replied in unison with Mom.

"Because they multiply by dividing."

The two laughed like they had just heard the joke. Mom reached over and touched Dad's face.

"I didn't wanna laugh, but he was cute, and I am a sucker for a man full of science jokes."

Franklin let out a chuckle drenched in pity. *They are so corny!* He felt a little better about his upcoming encounter with Danielle, though not by much. He sat back in his seat and leaned his head against the window. Dad looked at him through the rearview mirror. The light turned green, and he hit the gas as he began to speak.

"Franklin, you know..."

SCHREEEEEEEEEEEEEEEEEEEEEEEEEEEEEEEEEEECH!
CRASH!

No one ever saw the pick-up truck coming before it plowed into the side of the vehicle. The impact jerked Franklin's head to the right then immediately to left and it slammed against the glass window. He blacked out. He slowly opened his eyes to find his head pounded with pain and his vision blurry. He scanned the inside of the car. Dad was frightened but appeared to be otherwise unharmed. Mom was slumped into the deployed airbag. He blinked and when he refocused, he realized he had blacked out again.

"It's going to be okay, Franklin! I got you, son!" Dad screamed as he pulled him from the car.

Franklin gazed into the car through the door he had just been pulled out of. His vision was blurred but he could make out Brooklyn was slumped over into the seat he was just sitting in. She didn't move; neither did Mom.

On the other side of the car, he could see the front of the pick-up truck. Smoke bellowed from under the hood and its horn let out a constant, loud blare. He felt himself pass out again.

"Mom.......Brooklyn......."

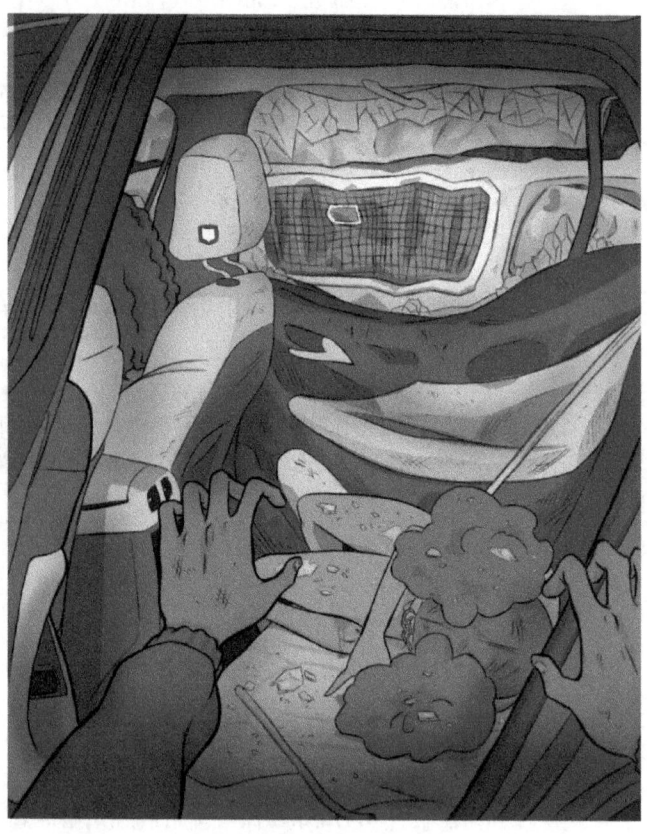

CHAPTER 3
A BAD DREAM

Franklin sat in a dark room, so absent of light that he couldn't see his hand in front of his face when he raised it. *What is going on? Why is it so dark in here?* Something touched his leg. He jumped.

"What was that?"

He was terrified, blinded by darkness, and he wasn't alone. Then he realized what he felt was a hand. The hand moved up his thigh in search for his. The hand was small and trembled as it moved. *Who is touching me?* He heard the hand's owner crying. He wanted to pull away, but whoever it was was just as scared as him.

"They are gonna take them! What are we going to do?"

It's a girl! She sounds young...but who is she talking about? They are going to take who? What is going on? And why is it so dark in here?

"Take who??! What are you talking about? And where are we?"

The little girl's sobs intensified.

"They are gonna take them and we are going to be all alone!"

"Take who?"

As his eyes adjusted to the darkness, Franklin could make out a small sliver of light on the floor in front of him and his unknown companion. The light came from underneath a door. They were being held captive. The sounds of footsteps could be heard approaching. The footsteps echoed as they drew closer. Franklin felt a knot in his stomach.

"They're coming!"

"Who's coming? What's going on?"

This had to be a mistake. Mom and Dad would never leave him in a dark room with some strange little girl. He had to call to them. He had to let them know he needed them.

"MOM! DAD! WHERE ARE YOU?"

"I told you...they are going to take them!"

"Take them? Mom and Dad?"

The footsteps intensified before finally coming to rest outside of the door. Franklin and the little girl fell silent. They both stared in the direction of the door, scared by what might be on the other side. Two voices began to speak just outside, but Franklin couldn't make out what was being said. Then, one voice shouted.

"Yes, Grand Inquisitor!"

Suddenly, the door slid open. Light poured into the room. Franklin shielded his eyes but could make out the silhouette of two tall figures. One of them began to walk away, its figure dissolved into the bright, white light. As he left, the figure spoke.

"Bring them to me."

On command, the other figure entered the room, the large, silhouetted frame blocked out the light. Franklin saw a hand reach for him.

"NOOOOOOOOOOOOOOOOOO!!!!!!"

Franklin woke up drenched in sweat. He had no idea where he was. His vision was blurry, and his head hurt. He heard muffled voices, but he couldn't make out what was being said. He tried to lift his head and sit up, but the drugs that coursed through his body wouldn't allow it. A voice that sounded familiar drew closer. He felt a hand on his forehead. It was Dad.

"Hey, buddy. You're awake! How are you feeling?"

Uncle Jason was there as well.

"Frankie...you're okay!"

Franklin attempted to talk, but his throat and mouth were dry. He examined his surroundings and realized he was in the hospital. The dark room, the scared, little girl, the man reaching for him...it was all a dream. He wasn't trapped in a room; he was in the hospital. The light green curtains were drawn and surrounded his bed.

Next to his bed was a chair; on the other side of it was another hospital bed, though its curtains were drawn. A soft light on the other side of the curtains allowed him to see through them. A continuous beeping sound echoed throughout the room. Rhythmic beeping.

Beep........Beep........Beep........Beep........

Dad poured ice water into a small, yellow plastic cup. He reached down and lifted Franklin's head and helped him sip the water. Franklin wasn't sure if he was still trapped in a dream.

"Dad. What happened?"

His throat and jaw hurt when he spoke.

"We were in a car accident, Franklin."

"A car accident?"

His eyes slowly regained focus and could see Dad's face more clearly. Dad's brow was wrinkled, not from anger, but from sorrow. His eyes were red. He had been crying. There was a bandage above his right eye. Uncle Jason turned his face away and wiped his eyes.

"Dad...what happened?"

Franklin slowly started to remember the morning's events; the accident, his head against the window, Mom slumped into the airbag.

"Dad, where's Mom?"

Dad sighed. "She is in the bed next to us. She is going to be okay."

Franklin sat up and looked at the curtain that divided his bed and the one next to him. Dad slowly walked over and slid the curtain back. It was Mom. She was asleep, a tube in her mouth, heavily bandaged around her head and bruises on her face. He counted no less than three machines hooked up to her that all beeped and flashed lights.

Beep........Beep........Beep........Beep........

His eyes welled up. Then he remembered the last thing he saw; Brooklyn slumped over in the car.

"Where's Brooklyn?"

Dad collapsed down into the chair next to his bed. Uncle Jason sniffled as he muffled his sobs.

"*BROOKLYN!* Where's Brooklyn, Dad!!?"

"Franklin, Brooklyn..."

"What, Dad? Where is Brooklyn? Is she okay?"

"Son, Brooklyn didn't..."

A lump formed in Dad's throat. He dropped his head into his hands and silently wept. He couldn't say the words. He couldn't bring himself to accept the truth, let alone relay it to Franklin. Franklin could sense something was horribly wrong.

"Franklin, Brooklyn didn't make it."

"Didn't make what?" he cried out as tears streamed down his face. "What are you saying? WHERE IS BROOKLYN?!"

"She died, Franklin. The truck hit the side of the car where she and your mother were. They tried to save her, Franklin. Her body just couldn't take it."

Dad trembled as he told Franklin his worst nightmare come true. He didn't want to believe it though. *No...NO! YOU'RE WRONG! Brooklyn is strong, super strong, much stronger than me! She didn't even cry last year when she broke her forearm riding her bicycle. She played a five-set tennis match with the flu! She can't die. Brooklyn is going to come walking through that door any moment, smile and point her finger at me and scream GOTCHA!*

He impatiently stared at the hospital room door. She never walked into the room.

41

"Nooooooooooooo, Dad! NOOOOOOO! Where is Brooklyn? Where is my sister, Dad?"

His sobs became uncontrollable.

"You're wrong! Brooklyn isn't dead! She can't be!!!"

Dad pulled himself together, got up and walked over to him. Dad did all he could do in that moment. He wrapped his arms around Franklin as Franklin struggled to understand why Brooklyn had to die. Uncle Jason pulled himself from his chair and joined them. He wrapped one arm around Dad and placed the other on Franklin's back. Franklin buried his head in Dad's chest and cried hard and loud. A doctor entered the room and interrupted their moment of grief.

"Excuse me, Mr. Williams. Can I talk to you in the hallway for a moment?"

Dad shook his head, gave a heartbroken look at Franklin, then looked back up at the doctor.

"Doctor, can you give me a moment?"

"I'm so sorry, Mr. Williams, but this is of extreme urgency."

The doctor darted his eyes towards Mom's bed, a signal to Dad that what he needed to share was about Mom and that Franklin probably shouldn't hear it. Dad reluctantly nodded.

"I'll be right outside, Franklin. Okay?"

The doctor walked out of the room. Dad rubbed his back, then placed his hand on his cheek and gave him a sorrowful, despondent look.

"I'll be right outside."

Uncle Jason joined Dad to talk to the doctor. Franklin laid back down. His world was turned upside down. His heart hurt in a way he never thought possible. He felt weak, drowsy and he couldn't stop crying. The medicine that coursed through his veins made his eyes heavy.

He didn't fight it. Maybe this was still a dream. Maybe he was still in that dark room. He would rather be there than in the hospital next to Mom. He would rather be scared in that room with the little girl than Brooklyn be gone. His blinks became longer as the medicine took over his body. *This is all a dream...*

Hours later he awoke. He woke up fully coherent and felt no effects from the drugs. The only light in the dark hospital room came from the soft, fluorescent light on the wall behind the bed next to him. He glanced to his left and saw Mom still unresponsive.

Beep........Beep........Beep........Beep........

Dad sat in the chair in between them. He held Mom's hand and stroked her hair. Franklin felt a sharp pain in his hand and saw there was an intravenous tube in his hand, connected to an I.V. bag hanging over top his bed. He was thirsty and searched for something, anything to drink. He took notice of a small, wheeled table in between the two beds. A beige cafeteria tray held what was supposed to be his dinner. He sat up, pulled the table close to him, and grabbed the small container of apple juice. As he peeled back the foil lid, Dad noticed his movements behind him.

"Hey, buddy. How are you feeling?"

"Is she really gone, Dad?"

43

"Yes, Franklin."

"And Mom?"

Dad sighed, stood up and walked close to Franklin's bed.

"We don't know yet, Frankie. The doctor told us she suffered a lot of damage to her skull and brain. Said the next few hours will be critical."

Dad tried to console him, tried to comfort him, but knew the best thing he could do is just be there. Franklin set his opened juice on the table, laid his face on Dad's chest, and wept silently, only the occasional sniffle indicated that he sobbed. His eyes affixed to Mom. She hadn't moved and appeared more like she was asleep, than in a medically induced coma.

Beep........Beep........Beep........Beep........

Dad kissed the crown of his head.

Franklin's eyes searched the room as he wept. Uncle Jason was gone.

"Dad, where's Uncle Jason?"

"He left. Seeing your mom like that was too much for him."

Franklin cried some more. Dad rubbed the back of his head.

"You have to be starving. I'll see if they can warm that tray up for you. Would you like that?"

Franklin nodded. Dad gave a halfhearted smile at him, then turned around, picked up the tray and walked

44

out of the room. Franklin laid back down and stared at the ceiling. He began to think about Brooklyn. Tears rolled down his face, their soft drops echoed in Franklin's ears as they landed on the hospital pillow. Suddenly, a nurse entered the room.

"Hello, Mr. Williams. It's time for your medicine."

Franklin stared at the nurse. He was an older man, slight of build, yet tall. There were strange tattoos on his forearms. Franklin had never seen a male nurse before. The nurse walked over to the side of his bed, reached into his pocket, and pulled out a syringe filled with a strange, green liquid. Franklin grew fearful.

"What is that?"

"This is something that will make you stronger!"

He inserted the point of the needle into the I.V. bag. Franklin now had an up close view of the man and his tattoos. They were strange symbols and words but written in a language unfamiliar to him.

"You may feel a slight burning sensation, Mr. Williams."

"OW! AH! AH! OWWWW!"

"Like I said, a slight burning sensation."

"What was that stuff?"

The nurse quickly removed the syringe, placed it into his pocket, and then walked to the foot of the bed. Suddenly, Franklin felt extremely sleepy. His veins felt as if they were on fire. He wanted to yell out, but whatever was coursed through him rendered him incapable of speech. He fought to keep his eyes open, he tried to focus

45

on the nurse. The nurse stood at the foot of the bed and watched him. As he drifted off to sleep, the last thing he saw was the nurse smile at him.

"Time to come home...... We need you."

Come home...?

Franklin woke up a few minutes later.

"Hey, buddy."

Dad was back with his dinner and had placed it on the rolling table. There was a female nurse in the room tending to the I.V. machine connected to his hand. She looked down at him and smiled.

"How are you feeling, Mr. Franklin?"

"Ok, I guess. That last shot put me to sleep."

Dad curiously glanced up at the nurse and saw her reaction. The nurse became confused by this revelation.

"Shot? What shot? You weren't scheduled for any medication outside of the ibuprofen Doctor McDowell prescribed for pain."

"Someone gave you a shot, son?

"It was a man. He was big and had tattoos. He gave me a shot with some green stuff in it."

The nurse giggled at the notion.

"A man? Green stuff? You may be imagining things, Franklin. That happens sometimes. You were under a pretty strong sedative earlier. Besides, we don't have any male nurses on call tonight."

He sprung to an upright position and snapped his head toward Dad.

"I'm serious, Dad. He was here!"

Dad was concerned, and wanted to believe him, but the nurse's story seemed more than plausible.

"Think you might've imagined that Buddy. I was only gone for two minutes and when I came back in, you were fast asleep."

Franklin was dejected. *I couldn't have imagined it! I remember the burning. I remember the nurse smiling at me.* He could *see* the male nurse as if he was still standing there. The female nurse placed her hand on his forehead.

"Why don't you try and eat something, Franklin? You have had one tough day. You need to eat and rest. In the morning, you'll forget all about this male nurse."

The nurse's eyes grew sympathetic. She flashed a sad smile at Franklin and Dad, gently touched Franklin's hand, and then left the room. Franklin didn't feel much like eating. He just decided to lay back down. He was confused and still in shock that Brooklyn was gone. He was scared Mom might die too. Dad crawled in bed next to him and held him.

As they laid there, Franklin wished he could fix it. He wished he could go back and stop it. He didn't care about seeing Danielle. He wanted to see Brooklyn. He would give anything for Brooklyn to be alive again. His heartbeat so hard he thought it might jump out of his chest. As much as he loved Dad, and appreciated Dad's comfort, he wanted to be alone.

47

"I need to go to the bathroom, Dad."

"Okay, son. Let me help you."

"I can do it."

"Franklin, you are still feeling the medication. Let me just..."

"I'm fine!   I just need to go to the bathroom...*please!*"

"Ok, Franklin. I'll be right here when you come out."

Franklin slowly crawled out of the bed. The cold air in the hospital room raced up his gown and gave him a chill. He reached out and grabbed the pole that held his IV for support, then wheeled it to the edge of the bed. He slowly shuffled his feet across the room and stopped at the bathroom door. He peeked back at Dad who had fearfully watched him the whole way. For the first time, he could see Mom's bed in full. She didn't move at all.

Beep........Beep........Beep........Beep........

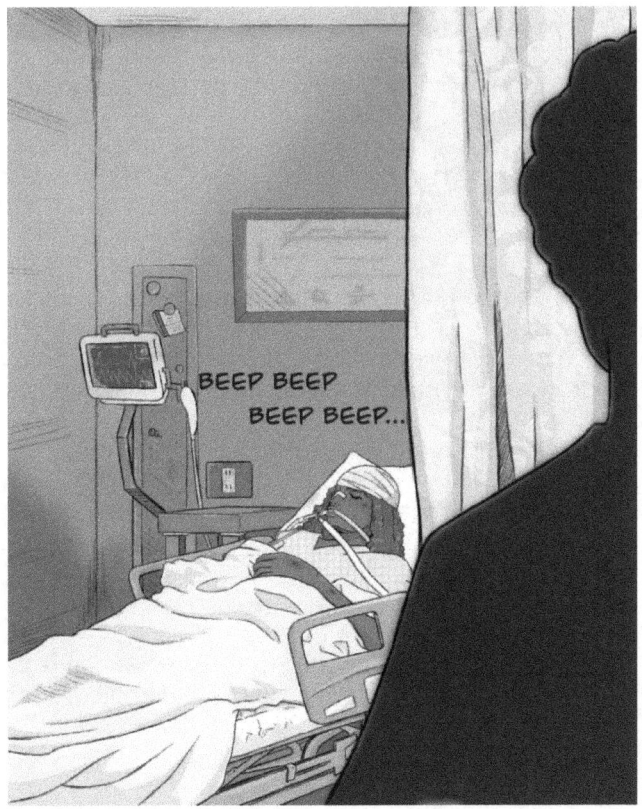

Franklin's head dropped down, he turned, entered the bathroom, and then shut the door behind him. He approached the sink and woefully stared into the mirror.

Why did you have to die, Brooklyn? Why? WHY? Is this my fault??? Did all of this happen because I didn't want to be a part of this family? Is it because of what I was thinking at breakfast? Brooklyn is gone, Mom is hurt, and I'd give anything for them to be okay. What did I do?

49

He began to tremble, not out of weakness or the side effects from the drugs, but out of grief and guilt. He wanted to go back. He wanted everything to just go back the way it was.

God, please don't take Mom too. PLEASE!! Please just make this a dream. I'm sorry! I take it all back! Just make things the way they were...PLEASE!!

He balled his fists up and his arms began to shake. He closed his eyes. His mouth was open, and though he wanted to scream, no sound came out. Then, he finally let out a loud, ear-piercing scream.

"AAAAAAAAAAAAAAAHHHHHHHHHHH!"

The room began to fill with light. Dad jumped out of the bed and ran to the bathroom to check on Franklin.

"FRANKLIN!"

The bright light in the room grew in intensity. Franklin continued to scream. He felt tingles all over his body. Then, it happened.

VLOOMP!

When he opened his eyes, he was standing in his room. His sneakers were on the floor next to him. It was morning time again. Panicked, his eyes scanned the room. *Am I dreaming? I was just in the hospital! I must be dreaming!*

"Breakfast!" shouted Mom.

Breakfast? What is going on?? He tried to make sense of it. If this was a dream, it felt too real. He could smell the turkey bacon and vegetarian eggs. He could hear sounds of Mom cooking downstairs. *You passed out again. Just wake up. Wake up. WAKE UP!*

"You ready to go suffer through this breakfast?"

Franklin snapped his head over to the bathroom door, and there she was. Brooklyn, with a huge smile as if nothing happened.

CHAPTER 4
REWIND

Franklin could hardly believe his eyes. Brooklyn stared back at him, taken aback by his reaction.

"What's wrong with you? Why are you staring at me like that?"

"I...I..."

"You...you what?" she mocked.

Franklin sprinted over and hugged her.

"Ewwww. Get off me, thank you."

He couldn't let her go. If this was a dream, he intended to hug her until he woke up. Tears of happiness flowed from his eyes, and he didn't want them to stop. Brooklyn squirmed, uncomfortable with such a strong display of affection from him.

"What is wrong with..." she cried out as she struggled to get him off, "...YOU?!"

She managed to break his vise like grip from around her and push him back into his room. She remained in the bathroom doorway and gawked at him as if he were crazy. Franklin quickly wiped the tears from his face. He wanted to explain everything to her but doubted she would believe him.

"You di....We were in a car accid...."

"*I what?* Why are you crying?!"

He used his shirt to wipe his eyes.

"Nothing. Nothing. I'm just happy you're okay."

"You're talking about yesterday, aren't you? Look, I'm sorry. I should've been there for your race. When I got back, you were already asleep. I didn't want to wake you."

Wait...did she say she wasn't there for my race? She was there! She was on the infield!

"What? You *were* there! We both were!"

"Franklin, I was at dance practice. I should have skipped it. I know how important that race was to you. But hey, you won, right?"

Franklin was confused.

"No, I didn't. I lost. *You* won."

"Franklin, are you sure you're okay?"

"Brooklyn! Franklin! Breakfast! We are having turkey bacon and vegetarian eggs!"

Franklin turned his surprised gaze towards the sound of Mom's voice. *That's what she said before. But how is everything with the race different? Why is Brooklyn saying she wasn't there?*

"Put your boots on and come on before she makes a vegetarian milkshake or something."

"Yeah. Yeah! Ummmm....let me finish getting ready."

"Oh yeah! Gotta look good for *Danieeeeelllllle.*"

Franklin could have cared less about seeing Danielle. He didn't want to go to the cookout anymore. He remembered Mom yelled for them to come eat breakfast the first time he experienced this.   He remembered her calling them by name the second time. He didn't look in the mirror and practice his lines for Danielle, so Brooklyn did things differently this time. *Why is she saying she was at dance practice? She gave up dance classes when she was eight! None of this is making any sense! As long as Dad doesn't call for us to come eat, then things should...*

"Kids! Get down here and eat this food your Mama cooked."

"Think he just doesn't wanna suffer alone?" asked Brooklyn.

Franklin's heart sunk. *I asked her that! What is going on? Is this all happening again, somehow?* Brooklyn shrugged her shoulders.

"Misery loves company, I guess. Come on, lover boy. Let's go get vegetarian eggs!"

She entered his room, then out of the door into the hallway. He followed behind her only to realize he wore nothing but socks on his feet. He turned back into the room and saw his boots by the door. He hurriedly slipped them on.

Just as before, Brooklyn started to race down the hallway to the stairs. When Franklin entered the hallway, he surveyed the walls in amazement. He saw pictures of him playing basketball, running track, diving for a ball in left field, the same as it was before. All of Brooklyn's photos were different. Pictures of her spiking a volleyball and receiving the baton for the anchor leg of a relay race were replaced by pictures of her leaping through the air in a leotard, and her dressed as an African princess as she twirled on one foot.

"Too slow!" she victoriously announced as she leapt off the stairs and landed with a thud.

"Now, are we gonna start this day with you two locked in mortal combat?" Mom asked.

"No, Mom. Franklin is scared today. He doesn't want these problems."

Brooklyn turned around with a triumphant look on her face. Franklin stood at the top of the stairs. He felt like he was in another world. *That was different. She didn't say that last time. Maybe if I change enough things, the accident won't happen.*

He slowly walked down the stairs and when he arrived in the kitchen, everything was exactly as he remembered it, everything except Dad. Dad wore a uniform, an Army uniform. He was a large man, with a wide chest and bulging biceps that filled out his uniform blouse. The Dad he knew was tall, but not nearly as muscular. Surprisingly, Dad's appearance was a welcomed change. He looked powerful and fearsome. *I never thought about Dad in the Army, but he looks like he was born for it!*

Mom once again, held a skillet in her hand as she hovered over the breakfast table and scooped large amounts of vegetarian eggs onto everyone's plates. Dad sat at the table, exactly as he did before (save for the uniform), his eyes wide as the large helping of unwanted eggs was placed on his plate. He dreadfully gazed at Franklin and Brooklyn, his eyes full of disgust. A pained smile grew on his face, a poor attempt to mask his true feelings.

"Come on, kids. Your Mama cooked us a healthy, *delicious* breakfast."

Brooklyn and Franklin stared at their father. Brooklyn's nose scrunched in disgust. Franklin couldn't take his eyes off of Dad's uniform. *Why is he in an Army uniform? What is going on?* Mom could tell something was bothering him.

"You okay, Franklin?"

"He is *tripping* today," answered Brooklyn as she sat down. "Mom, why do we have to eat this? You are the healthiest, fittest person we know. We can have some real food from time to time."

Franklin's eyes grew bigger. *I asked Mom that last time!* He soon realized that everything continued to play out as if it were meant to happen, no matter what he said or did differently.

"Well, we can always be healthier. Besides, we have a future Olympian and a world class dancer at the table. Got to fuel your bodies correctly. Isn't that right, Honey?"

Dad continued to eye his plate, just as he did before. Franklin's attention was affixed on Dad.

"Isn't that right, *Honey*?" Mom reasserted as she began to dig into her breakfast.

Dad winced then peeked at Franklin and Brooklyn, just as he did before. Franklin stared at his father, praying he wouldn't say "great fuel for the body."

"Oh, yes! Great fuel for the..."

"HEY, FAMILY!"

Uncle Jason burst through the back door, just as before. Franklin was stunned. *He is wearing a uniform too?!?!* Dad shook his head and returned to labor through breakfast. Uncle Jason scanned everyone's plate and scrunched his nose in disgust.

"What. Is. THAT?!?!"

"It's healthy, Jason," Mom remarked dismissively.

Uncle Jason turned his gaze to Franklin and Brooklyn.

"She gave you that 'future Olympians' line?"

Brooklyn giggled. Even Dad raised his eyebrows in agreement. Franklin sat with a blank expression. Mom was not amused.

"Jason, what do you want?"

"Dang, Sis. I can't even drop by and see the family? Besides, looks like I am saving these kids from malnutrition!"

"Jason, we are not having this discussion again."

Uncle Jason waved her off, pulled out a chair next to Mom and sat down. He grabbed a piece of turkey bacon and took a bite, then promptly spit it out into a napkin.

"Lord, woman! What are you doing to these kids?"

Brooklyn chuckled, then quickly quieted down when she saw the look on Mom's face. Franklin sat bewildered. They looked at each other, then down at their plates.

"I don't blame you, honestly," said Uncle Jason. "I remember when we were kids, your mom started drinking some wheat grass, barley root, pinecone breakfast mess."

"It was a high-protein whey shake," snapped Mom.

"It was a glass full of grass and dirt," quipped Uncle Jason. "And it didn't help her! She could never beat me!"

Uncle Jason burst out into laughter. Dad became annoyed, but before he could deliver the same positive affirmation of Mom's meal, Mom noticed Franklin's face.

"Franklin, are you sure you're okay this morning? You seem off," asked Mom.

"I'm fine, Mom. Can I be excused? I'm not all that hungry."

"Not until you have finished that food. Look, Brooklyn is enjoying it."

"That girl isn't enjoying that food! She is just trying to scarf it down!" Uncle Jason quickly interjected. "C'mon, Franklin. Let's go get some real food."

"No, he will sit right there like his mother told him to," scolded Dad.

Uncle Jason frowned, but quieted down. Franklin's head was on a swivel as the exchange played out. Then he noticed the rank insignias on their uniforms. Dad outranked Uncle Jason, and from the look of anger and embarrassment on Uncle Jason's face, he didn't like it. Uncle Jason rose from the table, then leaned over and kissed Mom on the crown of her head.

"Later, Sis."

"Where are you heading off to?" asked Mom.

"To the Pancake House to get some *real* food."

"You're not coming to the command picnic?"

"No, I am lead investigator on a case. It's a wild one! This Soldier decided he was going to..."

"Ahem!" interrupted Dad.

Uncle Jason stopped midsentence and let out a frustrated sigh.

"Y'all have fun. Later kids," Uncle Jason responded before glaring at Dad. "Colonel."

Dad never looked up from his plate.

"Major."

"Bye, Jason," replied Mom as she glanced over her shoulder before she turned her attention back to Franklin and Brooklyn. "Eat up! We have a busy day and a long drive to the cookout."

As Uncle Jason walked out the door, Franklin felt a rush of panic. *I need to talk to Uncle Jason. He wasn't at the accident. Maybe if I explain everything to him, he'll believe me. Maybe he'll know what I am supposed to do.*

"Mom, can I go and talk to Uncle Jason?"

"About what?"

About what?   About what??!   Think, Franklin. Think!!

"Ummmm...the race yesterday.   Wanted to talk about my form. He still holds all those school records and all."

Mom saw the anxiousness in Franklin's face and relented.

"Fine. Make it fast because we have a long drive ahead of us and you still have to finish your food."

Franklin leapt from the table. Brooklyn peeked at him as he bolted for the door, then continued to stuff food in her mouth until her cheeks bulged like a chipmunk.

"Brooklyn Rae Williams! Is that how a *lady* eats? Act like you have some home training and conduct yourself ..."

Mom's voice trailed off as Franklin ran through the back door. Uncle Jason sat atop his motorcycle and turned over the engine.

"UNCLE JASON!"

The purr of the motorcycle's engine drowned out his cry. *He can't hear me!* He began to sprint over to Uncle Jason just as he revved the engine. Uncle Jason kicked the kickstand out, revved the engine once more. *He is going to leave. Please wait!!* As he ran, time slowed down for Franklin. He ran faster and before he knew it, he was standing in front of Uncle Jason's bike.

"Where...How did you..?" exclaimed a startled and shocked Uncle Jason at Franklin's sudden appearance. He turned the motorcycle's engine off.

"Uncle Jason, I need to talk to you."

"Boy, I know you're fast, but how did you get from the kitchen table out here that fast??! It's like you appeared out of thin air!"

Franklin ignored the observation about how fast he arrived in front of Uncle Jason. He needed him to listen.

"Unc, something isn't right. Something is happening to me, and I don't know what to do or how to stop it."

"Franklin, I thought your dad had this conversation with you. You see, when a young boy starts his journey to manhood, sometimes there are feelings and changes to his body that..."

"No! It's not that!"

Franklin felt frustrated. *How do I explain that I know Brooklyn is gonna die and Mom is gonna be in a coma? How do I tell him that I am somehow going to end up in an alternate version of the day and have to relive all of it?* Uncle Jason became concerned.

"Franklin, are you okay? What's going on?"

Franklin sighed.

"It's just...something is going to happen if we go to that picnic. Something bad. Something is going to happen to Brooklyn."

Franklin thought he must sound crazy to Uncle Jason, but Uncle Jason didn't laugh. He didn't give him a patronizing look either. His head tilted, curious as to what Franklin could be attempting to tell him. He reached out and touched Franklin's shoulder.

"You're serious, aren't you?"

"I don't know what to do. Something bad is going to happen. We can't go to the picnic. If we do, Brooklyn is going to..."

"Frankie! Mom said it's time to go!"

Franklin and Uncle Jason turned to see Brooklyn lean out of the back door. She smiled at them.

"Mom said that since none of us liked what she cooked, we can just eat at the picnic. Let's go!"

She leaned back into the house and the door closed. Franklin turned back to Uncle Jason.

"We can't go, Unc!! We can't!"

"Frankie, I think you might be a little nervous about going. Isn't your little girlfriend going to be there?"

"It's not about her! I swear!! It's Brooklyn. She is going to..."

Suddenly, Dad's voiced echoed from the front of the house.

"Sounds good to me!"

Oh no! That's what he said before. Uncle Jason started his engine again and gently pushed Franklin out of the way.

"Frankie, we will talk about this tonight. Nothing is going to happen, trust me. But right now, I gotta go. Love you, dude."

Franklin almost cried as he watched Uncle Jason ride off. *But it is. I just know it and I can't stop it!!*

"Franklin! Let's go, son!" shouted Dad from the front of the house.

Franklin ran around the side of the house to meet the family. They were already in the car. He sprinted to the passenger side door where Mom sat. Her window was down.

"Mom, we can't go."

"Are you nervous about Danielle?" asked Dad as he leaned over to see through Mom's window.

"No. I don't care about Danielle!"

"Franklin!" shouted Mom incredulously.

Franklin ignored Mom's chastisement and turned his attention to Brooklyn. Brooklyn was shocked by Franklin's behavior.

"Brooklyn, get out of the car! We can't go!"

"Sounds to me like you're nervous, Franklin," Dad observed. "Trust me. Everything is going to be fine."

No, it's not!!! All we need is a few seconds. Just a few seconds to be off. If we are a few seconds late, then the truck won't hit us. Think! What can I change??

"Ummmm..."

He quickly shot his eyes down and saw his boots. *That's it!!! Last time I wore boots, but I was going to wear sneakers!*

"I need to change my boots! I want to wear my sneakers."

Brooklyn laughed.

"For what?? You'll still look like a toddler! Did Mom pick out that outfit for you, little boy?"

"Get in the car," reassured Mom. "You look amazing."

"Mom don't lie to that boy. He looks like a toddler!"

"Brooklyn!"

Franklin sulked and fought back tears. He slowly walked over to the seat behind Dad, opened the door, and reluctantly climbed in. Dad started the engine, and off they went. Brooklyn placed her ear pods in her ears and began to listen to music, just as before. Franklin watched Dad tune to sports talk radio, just like he remembered.

Time seemed to move in slow-motion. Mom reached into her purse, pulled out her tablet, and began to read her book. Franklin was too nervous to do anything other than think of what was about to happen next. He reached for his phone, then remembered that's what he did last time, so he slid it back in his pocket. Mom's intuition must have gone haywire. She paused in her reading and turned around to look at Franklin.

"Relax, baby. Danielle is a nice girl. Smart, too. She would be a fool not to like you."

Mom always had a way of making him feel better, but this time, she was way off base. He stared at her; his face gripped in fear. He could still hear the beeps.

Beep........Beep........Beep........Beep........

Dad peaked at him through the rearview mirror as they approached a stoplight. As he eased into the breaks, he began to speak.

"It's okay to be nervous, Franklin. Just relax and be yourself, son."

Franklin feverishly scanned the intersection as his father spoke. He didn't see any cars coming. No one noticed the pick-up truck that turned out of the gas station across the street and to their right. It pulled out like a drag race car would, its driver recklessly sped down the road to catch the light before it turned red. It was too late, however. The light began to change from green to yellow. The driver accelerated.

VRRRROOOOOOOOOOOOMMM!!!

The driver's light turned red. Dad's light turned green. As Dad began to pull off, he peeked at the rearview mirror once again.

"You know, Franklin..."

SCHREEEEEEEEEEEEEEEEEEEEEEEEEEEEEEEEEECH!

This time, Franklin was ready. As the pick-up truck careened towards the side of their vehicle, his worst nightmare unfolded. He wanted to save them both, Mom and Brooklyn. He knew Mom survived the accident before, maybe she would again. But Brooklyn wouldn't. Visions of the hospital room flashed in his mind. The memory of hearing Brooklyn died. Seeing Mom in the hospital bed. The beeps.

Beep........Beep........Beep........Beep........

He had to react! He saw everything play out in slow motion. *Maybe if I pull her away from the window, she can survive!* Franklin reached out for Brooklyn with both hands, grabbed her by the arm and screamed.

"BROOKLYN!!!"

VLOOMP!

There was a bright flash. He was blinded and felt tingles all over his body, but neither were as disorienting as the last time. When his eyes adjusted, he saw they were in a park, not too far from where they lived. What had him disoriented this time wasn't the flash, or the tingles, or the fact he was no longer in the car. What had his mind boggled were his hands: they still held Brooklyn's arm.

"Uuuuhhhh," she painfully cried out. She still felt the effects of the jump. "What happened?"

Oh! My! God! I saved her! She stood right in front of him, alive, disoriented, but alive. She struggled to make sense of how one moment they were in the family car and the next they were in the park they played in as kids.

"Franklin, where are we? What happened?"

He didn't know how to explain it. He was just happy that she was alive. He began to look around. He breathed heavily, his heart pounded, and he had no answers. He only had one question, the same question that ran through Brooklyn's mind:

How did we get here?

CHAPTER 5
BROOKLYN DAZE

"Franklin, where are we?"

He helplessly looked at Brooklyn, then the surrounding area. They were in the playground, not too far from their house. They had played more times than they could count as children. *How did we end up here? Why here?*

"It's the playground. Near the house, I think."

"I know it's the playground!" Brooklyn chided. "How did we get here??"

The Brooklyn he knew would have punched him. Her temper was renown. This Brooklyn seemed genuinely terrified. It was the first change in her he welcomed.

"Let me explain."

"Let you explain? *Let you explain?!?*"

He stepped back. *No, she is like my Brooklyn. She is about to lose it. She's gonna say this is all my fault...and she's right.*

"Look, I know this is going to sound crazy..."

"Crazy? One minute we were in the car with Mom and Dad, the next minute we are at the playground! Crazy? This is *beyond* crazy!!!"

"Calm down, Brook."

"Don't 'calm down Brook,' me! What is going on?? And since when do you call me Brook??! You know I hate that!"

She collapsed down onto the grass. Franklin scanned the playground once again; it was empty, save for two little boys that had stopped playing on the monkey bars and were now staring at them. *Did they see us just appear here? I need to calm her down. Guess I'll have to try and explain this to her.* He sat down on the grass next to her and placed his arm around her. He took a deep breath then began to try and make everything make sense to her. It hardly made sense to him, but he had to tell her something.

"This is going to sound crazy, but here it goes..."

Franklin told her his amazing tale. How the Brooklyn he knew was the best athlete in the city. He recounted the accident and that she died. That Mom was in a coma. The mystery nurse that injected him with the green serum. He held back tears as he explained how he was angry she was gone. He told her about screaming in the bathroom, and the next thing he knew, he was back in his bedroom this morning. How the Dad he knew wasn't in the Army. Neither was Uncle Jason. How though things were different, the events repeated as before, and that the accident happened again.

His tears finally escaped his eyes and streamed down his face as he explained what raced through his mind seconds before they ended up in the playground. All he wanted to do was save her and Mom, but he couldn't save them both. Mom would survive, but she wouldn't.

"I just wanted to pull you away from the door. I wanted to keep you safe. I couldn't lose you again. But somehow, we ended up here."

Brooklyn stared off into space. He figured it was because she was in shock. *Please believe me, Brook. Please.* Finally, Brooklyn returned her harsh scowl to Franklin and shook her head in disbelief.

"You're crazy!"

"I know, it sounds crazy."

"No. You *are crazy!* You expect me to believe that I died, and you can travel in time?? That I am not the sister you've known your entire life??"

"I don't understand it either, Brook...I mean Brooklyn."

She stood up, dusted the dirt and loose grass off her sweatpants, and then stared down at him. The scowl on her face hurt him. It was the same look of disdain and anger *his* Brooklyn gave him on the track the day before.

"What I understand is you are completely nuts! Like psycho ward, need to be institutionalized, 'I need heavy medication' nuts!"

Franklin sighed. *She never believes me.* Brooklyn realized she still had her cellphone. She unlocked it and pushed the screen angrily. Franklin knew what she was doing. *She is calling Mom and Dad.* She placed the phone to her ear then immediately grunted.

"Great! No signal!"

Franklin pulled his phone out as well. *No bars? Why aren't our cells working?*

71

Brooklyn backed away from him, turned around, and stormed off. Franklin watched in frustration as she left.

"Brook!"

"AAARRRHHHGGGG!!!"

He shook his head as he got up and began to chase her. *Gonna be hard not to call her that.*

"Brooklyn! Where are you going?"

"Home! Home to Mom, Dad, and the land of the sane people!"

Her voice cracked as she spoke, then she wiped her face and picked up her pace.

"Brook...Brooklyn, I know you're scared. Please don't cry."

"I'M NOT CRYING! I just want Mom and Dad!"

To argue with Brooklyn in this state was pointless. When *his* Brooklyn had her mind made up about what she was going to do, there was no stopping her. *I can't blame her. Guess I'd be mad and confused too.* He decided to just follow her in silence. Suddenly, she stopped. *Thank God! She may not run track, but she is still fast!* Brooklyn turned around and stared at him. Her eyes were full of anger and her fists were balled up.

"I died, Franklin? Really?! That's *funny* to you? You pick on me all the time! But this?? THIS?!?!?"

"Pick on you???"

"YES! And now somehow you have me here telling me I died. You are unbelievable!!!"

"No!!! I was devastated," he whispered, his head down and his eyes welling with water.

"Are you crying? You're actually crying? You are really trying to sell this crazy lie you're telling, huh?"

"But it isn't a..."

She didn't stay to let him finish. She turned around and ran.

"...lie."

Franklin ran behind her as they traveled through their neighborhood. The route home troubled him, and he started to slow down. *Everything is different.* The grocery store on Chamberlain Street wasn't a grocery store, it was a hardware store. The string of new houses that lined Fountain Avenue were gone, replaced by a gathering of tall trees that stood in their place.

When they made it to the corner of Fulton Street and Ralph Avenue, Brooklyn finally slowed down. She stared at the gas station across the street. This was the gas station Dad stopped at every morning to get his newspaper and coffee. It was the same gas station, but it looked new. The sign above the gas station's awning that covered the gas pumps read GRAND OPENING. Franklin chalked it up to another thing that didn't make sense. Brooklyn seemed bothered by it as well.

"Franklin, why does that sign say grand opening?"

This surprised him. *So, this is different for her too!*

"I don't know," he replied.

73

Brooklyn was stunned as she scanned the gas station.

"It looks brand new, like they literally just opened, and I know for a fact that gas station has been there for as long as I can remember."

"The houses over on Fountain were gone, too."

Brooklyn's brow wrinkled.

"There were never houses there."

Franklin shook his head. "Of course not."

Though Franklin's story started to become plausible to Brooklyn, she still didn't want to believe it. *I must be going crazy, as crazy as him!* She took off again, crossed Fulton Street, and then turned down Hancock Street, the street that they lived on. Her pace slowed down as she looked at Hancock Street. The tall trees that lined their block looked smaller. The Garcia's house was a deep blue color instead of forest green, like she always knew it to be. Even the cars that lined the driveways were different; some were different makes and models, others were the same cars they always knew to be there, except they were newer. There was one vehicle that stuck out more than other's: Dad's.

It wasn't the red sedan they rode in that morning. It was an old, blue minivan. Brooklyn remembered riding in it when she was four. Franklin finally caught up to Brooklyn who now stood at the edge of the driveway and stared at the vehicle. Franklin looked at her, then at the minivan.

"Franklin, why is the old minivan in the driveway?"

"Whose is it?"

74

"You don't remember? That was ours!"

He had never seen it before. Then he had a realization. *People aren't the only thing different. It's like this whole world is different. But at least she is seeing it too. We BOTH can't be crazy!*

"Ummmm...." he replied, unsure of how to explain it.

"Let me guess, you remember us having a different one."

Franklin shrugged his shoulders to which Brooklyn sucked her teeth, rolled her eyes, then approached the house. The full rose bushes that lined the front of the porch were there, just as Franklin remembered, but they were small saplings. The planter boxes outside of the windows Mom had Dad put in just last summer were absent.

Confused, the two siblings slowly walked up the stairs of the porch. The stain looked fresh, not worn after years of wear and tear like he was used to. Brooklyn went to ring the doorbell, but Franklin saw something through the open blinds of the living room window. He grabbed her forearm and pulled her towards him.

"Wait. Look!"

She walked over to see what had alerted him. They crouched down and hid below the windowsill. They saw Dad. He sat in the living room, but everything about him was different. His shiny, bald head was replaced with a full head of hair. His facial hair was styled in a thin, well-manicured goatee and not the full beard Franklin remembered nor the clean-shaven military grooming that Brooklyn was accustomed to. Then, they heard Mom call out as she made her way downstairs.

75

"Baby! Can you help me with this?"

She appeared at the bottom of the stairs; a large bag pressed up against her chest. Mom was different as well. Her hair was shorter and cropped into a curly Mohawk. Dad set his paper down and ran over to her.

"Honey, what are you doing? You know you shouldn't be carrying that in your condition."

"I know, but I wanted to get rid of all that stuff in that bedroom. We have to make room for the baby."

Franklin and Brooklyn turned to each other and silently mouthed the word "baby." They looked back just as Dad took the bag from Mom and revealed her huge belly, full of child.

"Franklin, what's going on?"

Franklin didn't reply.

"Come over here," Dad said to Mom in a protective, nurturing voice. "Sit. I'll take care of this."

Mom slowly walked over to the couch in the living room in a gentle waddle. Franklin recognized the couch. As a child, he loved curling up next to Mom to snuggle on it. He was sad when they got rid of it three years ago.
"I miss that couch."

"I've never seen it before," whispered Brooklyn.

Nothing surprises me anymore. He returned his gaze to Mom. He was glad to see her awake and alive, not like he saw her in the hospital.

Beep......Beep......Beep......Beep......

76

Mom placed one hand on the armrest of the couch, and slowly lowered herself into a comfortable position. Dad re-entered the room, having gotten rid of the bag Mom once carried, and sat down next to her. He placed his arm around her as she leaned back into him and rested on his chest. With his other hand, Dad rubbed her stomach and smiled.

"Can you believe we are about to have a baby?"

"I have been carrying this baby for the last thirty weeks. If anyone knows we are having a baby, I do."

They both laughed, then Mom turned her head and looked back at him. They kissed, smiled at each other, then kissed again.

"A girl. I am gonna be a father," he said with a smile. "Daddy's little girl."

"Mmmm hmmm. And you are gonna spoil her rotten!"

"Of course, I am! She is gonna walk up and say 'Daddy, can I have ice cream for breakfast?' and I am gonna say 'Of course you can,'...wait, we still don't have a name for her."

"I thought we settled on Breanna?"

Dad shook his head vigorously.

"After your Aunt Breanne?? Oh no! That woman was crazy! Never liked me in life and I am not about to invite that spirit back up in here!"

"Well, what do you want to name her? Please don't say Claire."

"What's wrong with Claire?"

"So, because you still hold a childhood crush on the mom from a TV show, we are supposed to name her Claire? Nope. Not in my house."

"Well, we have time."

Franklin and Brooklyn backed away from the window. Brooklyn finally accepted that Franklin might not be crazy after all. As they descended the stairs, Franklin began to contemplate their situation.

If Mom is pregnant with a girl, it has to be Brooklyn. But how? Did I jump back in time? Is that what I have been doing?

"Franklin," Brooklyn stated in an eerily calm voice as they made it to the sidewalk and headed back for the park.

But if we have leapt back in time, and Mom is pregnant with Brooklyn, isn't that breaking some sort of space-time, future rules?

She glanced over at him and saw he was lost in thought.

"Franklin."

I have seen every time travel movie there is. It can't be possible for that to be Brooklyn. I mean, there can't be two Brooklyns, can there?

"Franklin!"

But there was that one movie where the guy was in the hot tub and...

78

"FRANKLIN!!!!"

Franklin jumped. "Huh? My bad. I was trying to figure out..."

"Was that *our* mom and dad?"

"I think so. Yeah, that was them."

"And Mom is pregnant?"

"Yes."

"With a girl?"

"Yeah, it appears so, but it doesn't make sense.

"Franklin."

"Yes, I think that's you in there or maybe it isn't," he replied in a calm tone that angered Brooklyn. "I'm just as confused as you."

"Franklin!"

"Yes?"

She abruptly stopped walking, turned and glared at him.

"You should pray. Pray this is a dream and I am going to wake up in the car when we get to the command party."

He pitifully stared back at her. He wished all of it was a dream too.

"Because if this is real, I am going to have to kill you."

79

"I know."

They continued their journey in silence. They passed the wrongly painted houses and the "new" old cars. They passed the newly opened gas station they had frequented for years. They passed the string of trees where houses should be and the furniture store where they normally buy milk, bread, and chicken. They walked in silence for the ten or so blocks until they arrived back at the park. Brooklyn stopped at the exact spot they arrived at and turned to Franklin.

"Okay."

"Okay what?"

"Do it!"

"Do *what?*"

"Do your thing! Your time magic or whatever you call it."

"That's the thing..."

"Franklin Connor Williams! If you tell me you don't know how you did it, so help me God...no, so help *you* God, I really *am* gonna kill you!"

He recoiled his body and shrugged his shoulders, his face turned up and his eyebrows raised.

"OH! MY! GOD! FRANKLIN!!!"

"I'm sorry! First time I did it was in the hospital after you died. I just wanted you to be alive. Then I appeared back in my room this morning like the accident never happened. The second time it happened is when we were in the car, right before the truck hit us! I just reached out and grabbed your arm and POOF! We were here!"

Brooklyn laughed, then sat down in the grass.

"This is crazy! No, I'm going crazy. Yup!! I've gone crazy. I am probably doped up, strapped to a table or in a padded room in the mental ward."

While Franklin and Brooklyn argued over time travel and their current states of sanity, a man in an all-black suit, watched from across the street. He stood far enough away as not to draw attention and watched Franklin and Brooklyn from the moment they returned to the park. He had a device in his hand, and had been waving it in the air, but he stopped when they arrived. While Brooklyn continued her rant, the man approached. Franklin noticed the man drawing near. *Who is this?* He nudged his sister.

"Brooklyn."

"Please, don't run," he said, his arms extended in front of him. "I mean you no harm."

Brooklyn immediately jumped to her feet and pushed Franklin behind her. Even though he was taller and slightly heavier than her, she always tried to protect him. It must be a trait Brooklyn has no matter *where* or *when* she is. As the man drew closer, Franklin began to examine him closer.

He was a tall, thin, older man, with a cleanly shaven head yet neglected the stubble of his beard. He hadn't shaved in days. His suit sagged on his body, like it was his older brother's suit, and he just played make believe like he was an actual grown up.

Franklin noticed his untucked white shirt and hastily knotted tie. He had a desperate smile on his face, as if their miraculous appearance offered him some sort of pleasure. There was a familiarity to him that intrigued Franklin. *Why do I know him?*

"Who are you?" demanded Brooklyn.

"I am someone that can help you."

"We don't need your help," a wary Franklin said as he stepped from behind Brooklyn.

"You sure about that? You're not from here, are you?"

The siblings looked at each other, then back at the man.

"Yes, we are," Brooklyn defiantly replied. "We live just around the corner!"

The man looked in the direction she pointed in, dropped his head, and began to shake it. He saw the direction that they came from and knew Brooklyn was lying. Franklin read his reaction. *Brook never was a good liar. I didn't even believe that.* The man stared at the two of them and an excited grin crept across his face. Brooklyn and Franklin didn't understand why he was smiling. Then, he spoke.

"No. I didn't mean you're not from this place. I meant, you're not from *this time*, are you?"

CHAPTER 6
THE MAN IN BLACK

"How did you know we aren't from here?" asked a surprised Brooklyn.

The man's eyes widened, and a huge smile burst upon his face from an explosion of excitement.

"So, it's true! Tell me, what year are you from? Is it the past? No, has to be the future!"

Brooklyn was having none of it.

"We aren't telling you anything until you tell us who you are and how you know anything about us?"

Franklin stared at the man's face. He wasn't as cautious of the man as Brooklyn was. For some reason, Franklin felt he could trust him. *I've seen him before, but where?*

"Mister, why do you think we are from the future? Who are you?" asked Franklin.

"I'm sorry. My name is Dr. Monroe Classon. I am a...I *was* the lead scientist for a company working on a revolutionary formula that... Look, I will tell you two everything, but we have to go!"

"We??" they responded in unison.

"We are not going anywhere with you, Mister," snapped Brooklyn defiantly.

Franklin became worried when the man's excitement quickly dissipated. Dr. Classon swiveled his head the way a fearful gazelle would of an approaching lion. His eyes remained wide, but they read of fear. His worry caused Franklin to look around as well. *What is he scared of?*

"Who are you looking for?"

"We don't have time. Please, come with me."

Dr. Classon extended his hand towards Brooklyn to bring her along with him. Brooklyn retreated from him just as fast.

"No! We don't even know you!"

"If I know you're here, that means they do too. Now *please,* come with me!"

"Who is they?" she asked again before turning to Franklin. "Let's get away from this man."

Suddenly, Franklin, Brooklyn, and Dr. Classon heard an engine rev in the distance. The engine's roar grew louder and louder.

"Too late! They're here! Come with me if you want to know what's going on!"

Dr. Classon ran right between them, through the park, and stopped by an old, dinged, gray van. He slung the door open and shouted.

"Get in!"

The car was closing in on them. It was an all-black sedan, with tinted windows. Franklin could see two men inside through the windshield. *This isn't good!* Panicked, he sprinted towards the van.

"Come on, Brook!"

She didn't respond. Brooklyn stood frozen with fear. The black sedan was closing in. He ran back to her, grabbed Brooklyn by the hand and yanked her arm.

"Come on!"

Brooklyn snapped out of her stupor and followed him. They arrived at the van seconds later. Brooklyn climbed in first, Franklin right on her tail, then he slammed the sliding door shut behind him. Dr. Classon was already in the driver's seat and was about to start the engine. Franklin noticed he was wearing a set of protective earmuffs.

"How do you expect to outrun that car in this beat up, old thing?"

"And what's with the earmuffs?" inquired Brooklyn.

Dr. Classon simply smiled.

"Cover your ears and buckle up!"

When Dr. Classon turned the ignition, the van let out a thunderous roar, louder than anything Franklin or Brooklyn had ever heard before. Their bodies vibrated as the engine rumbled, and the dashboard lit up like something out of a science-fiction movie. They quickly buckled their seat belts, then placed their hands over their ears. When Dr. Classon stepped on the accelerator, the van took off from its standing position so fast, they were thrown back into their seats and could hardly breathe.

"WHAT IS THIS THING?" shouted Franklin.

"I told you, I'm a scientist!" Dr. Classon yelled back over his shoulder.

The two men in the car glanced at each other, then the driver floored the pedal, determined to catch them. Dr. Classon caught a glimpse at the side mirror. The men were gaining on them. Dr. Classon smiled.

"Think you can catch me, huh?"

He reached towards the center panel and hit one of the many buttons that were lit up. It was then that Franklin noticed a computer screen below the panel of buttons and switches.

"Calculating," announced a computerized, female voice.

Franklin and Brooklyn glanced at each other, both terrified by the reckless speed they travelled at. Franklin's eyes fixed in on the computer screen. There was a 3-dimentional rendering of the van, with bar graphs labeled "FUEL", "POWER", "THRUSTERS", amongst others. *Thrusters? Why does this van have...?* Suddenly the screen changed to a 3-dimensional map. *What is this thing calculating?*

"Optimal path model, complete," the computer informed. "Shall I execute?"

The computerized voice was the only calm voice in the van. Dr. Classon howled with glee. Brooklyn screamed. Franklin was scared as well, but he was more worried about what would happen next. *Execute what?* He would soon get his answer.

"Yes!" shouted Dr. Classon, then he took his hands off the wheel and unbuckled his seatbelt.

"Auto-pilot engaged.   Hyper-sonic driving mode commencing in 5..."

Dr. Classon leaned out of the window.

"What are you doing?! GET BACK IN HERE! Put your hands on the wheel!!" screamed a terrified Brooklyn.

"...4..."

Dr. Classon ignored Brooklyn's pleas. He flashed a huge smile at the men in the car. The two men stared back at him in utter surprise, confused how the car was being driven if the driver was leaning out the window, smiling at them.

"...3..."

Dr. Classon waved at them.

"...2..."

He quickly sat back into his seat and tightened his seatbelt. Franklin and Brooklyn fumbled as they attempted to tighten their belts as well.

"...1..."

"Hold on!!"

Franklin and Brooklyn grabbed each other's hand, both squeezing as tight as they could. Then the computer spoke.

"Engage."

A low hum slowly built into an almost ear-piercing tone before it fell silent for a split-second.

"Heeeere weeeeeee..."

BOOM!

"...GOOOOOOOOO!!!!"

The van shot off like a rocket. It deftly weaved in and out of traffic, avoided every car with precision, and ran every traffic signal. Franklin and Brooklyn didn't see any of it though. Their eyes were tightly shut as both screamed like never before. Dr. Classon squealed with excitement. After a few seconds, the van's hum slowly began to wind down as the van decelerated. When it finally came to a stop, neither Franklin nor Brooklyn moved. They were frozen like statues. They slowly opened their eyes to see Dr. Classon staring at them with a huge smile on his face, like an eager child wanting to open a present.

"Everybody okay?"

Brooklyn feverishly undid her seat belt, slung the door open and leaned her head out of the van to vomit. Franklin turned his face up at the sight of it as he climbed out of the van. Dr. Classon climbed out of the van and slammed the door behind him.

"I can't believe that worked!"

Shocked, Franklin and Brooklyn both turned to look at him.

"YOU CAN'T BELIEVE THAT WORKED??!"

"Well, yeah. I mean, in all the simulations I've done, there was a ninety-eight-point-five percent probability it would work!"

Brooklyn reoriented herself after emptying her stomach.

"So, let me get this straight, you almost killed us, we are running from two men that act like they want to kill us, and all of this happened because my brother sucked me back in time...after I died?

"You could have killed us, Doc!" Franklin echoed.

"But I didn't! That was amazing!"

91

Dr. Classon still had the biggest smile on his face. Franklin noticed he got excited like a kid his age would. He was hyper, talked fast and was in a constant state of movement.

Franklin and Brooklyn began to take in their surroundings. The area they were in was oddly familiar to Franklin. *This is the New Warehouse District! But where are the stores, and the restaurants, and offices?* It was a desolate and barren place, full of old, worn down warehouses, many of which were abandoned.

"Where are we?" asked Brooklyn.

They were in front of a warehouse. On top of the building was an old, faded sign that "DENTON CHEMICALS". Dr. Classon walked over to the mailboxes that were mounted onto the brick wall.

"My place."

He reached inside one of the mailboxes deeper than his arm should have been able to travel. Suddenly, the thick, metal gate that closed the loading dock began to slowly creep open. He got back into the van and smiled at Franklin and Brooklyn. They both thought he was completely out of his mind. He motioned his head towards the loading dock gate.

"Just follow me in. Hurry though. That gate will start to close as soon as I'm inside."

As the van slowly crept into the dark space the gate revealed, Franklin cautiously followed. Brooklyn remained outside.

"Brook..."

Her eyes squinted as she glared at him with anger.

"My bad. Brooklyn, you can't stay out here."

"The man is crazy, Franklin. Doctor or no doctor."

"Maybe, but he *is* the one that just saved us."

She folded her arms and turned away from, the tell-tale sign that she was not up for reason. *There's the Brooklyn I know and love.* He tried anyway.

"That gate closes and you're out here by yourself."

The van cleared the gate's path, and just as Dr. Classon foretold, it started to roll down. The sound of the gate motor prompted a reluctant Brooklyn into action. She let out a grunt and darted into the warehouse, ducking as the gate made its way back down. As the light from outside faded away, the warehouse became darker. Just before the final sliver of natural light was extinguished, Dr. Classon flipped a switch, and the overhead lights illuminated the dark space in spurts.

There were eight hanging lights, though only three were operational, each highlighting a different environment. One lit up the space immediately to their right. The light shone down like an inverted cone, and highlighted an old, wooden bed in the center. The bed wasn't made and there were random clothes thrown about. A solitary lamp sat atop what Franklin assumed was a metal drum. To their left, was a small dining room table with a single chair. A small refrigerator, the kind one would see in a hotel room, rested next to a table. On top of it, was a portable cooktop, and mismatched dishes, bowls, and cups.

The light in front of them illuminated a small laboratory. A long metal table was covered with beakers, flasks, and Bunsen burners, all filled with colorful fluids. Franklin focused on Dr. Classon as he scurried around the space. *Is he some sort of mad scientist or something?* Just behind the metal table were two desks, smashed together to form one huge one. The desk held six computer screens, some suspended in air by metal poles. They were arranged in such a manner that if a person sat in front of them, they would be surrounded by them.

"You two hungry? I have some old tuna in the fridge."

"No," responded Franklin. "Doc?"

"Yes."

"Can you please tell us what is going on?"

"Right! That part. So, ummmm....here. Have a seat."

Underneath the metal table covered in chemistry equipment and colorful fluids, were two stools. Dr. Classon pulled them out and offered them to Franklin and Brooklyn. He frowned and placed his hand on his chin and rubbed his stubble.

"Where to begin?"

"From the top would be nice," Brooklyn replied.

"Right! What do you know about biochemistry and molecular structure?"

They didn't respond.

"Right! Nothing. Okay, so the company I used to work for was on the cutting edge of something remarkable. My team and I had developed a way to not only impart any trait we wanted into an organism at the molecular level, but the serum we created was the perfect vehicle to use to introduce medicines to an organism at a level that was unprecedented. The applications were endless. Imagine! Being able to attack cancer or Alzheimer's at the cellular level and deliver nutrients or medicines to that cell that either cured the problem or forced it and *only* it to die!"

"We knew were on to something big. Then the powers that be wanted to sell it to the highest bidder. That's when the government got involved. They wanted us to develop a way to make soldiers stronger, healthier. We were to look at what each participant was deficient in and introduce that to their cell structure using the serum. Initially, we saw no tangible results. It was the third test subject that gave us our first breakthrough. He had developed a rare form of skin cancer."

"We didn't know too much about him, other than he was one of the best snipers in the world and the military didn't want to lose him. I developed a protein-based medication that fed the dying, cancer riddled cells in his skin, causing them to regenerate at a rate faster than the cancer could kill them. We injected him and the initial findings were promising."

Dr. Classon's face grew tense. His brow wrinkled and he paused for a few seconds before he continued.

"A few days after we injected him, he died. I decided to perform an autopsy on him. When I went to cut his abdomen, I couldn't."

"What do you mean you couldn't?" a puzzled Franklin asked.

"I mean I couldn't. The scalpel's blade literally could not cut his skin. The skin was soft, pliable, and appeared to be perfectly healthy to the naked eye. I set the metal scalpel down and got out the laser scalpel. I'm telling you; I had the laser on his skin so long, I should have burned a hole right through him. Nothing. Not a scratch, a burn, nothing!"

"So, what are you telling us?"

"His skin had become impervious to intrusion."

"English, Doc," prompted Franklin.

"In essence, he became bulletproof. I know he was bulletproof because we shot him."

"You shot a corpse?" a disapproving, yet shocked Brooklyn asked.

"It was for science! But the problem we now had was, we did something remarkable, but since his skin couldn't be cut, we couldn't even see how his skin had changed. When word got out about our findings, men with well-pressed, military uniforms, covered in colorful medals arrived in my lab. They wanted us to do it again. Thing was, we didn't know how we did it in the first place! We ran test after test and got nothing. That was until subject number seven."

Franklin continued to listen, but his mind continued to drift back to Dr. Classon's familiarity. *I know I've seen him before. But how? If I am in the past, how could I possibly know him?* Dr. Classon continued.

"Subject number seven, Captain Santiago. He had been badly burned over seventy percent of his body from an I.E.D. explosion while leading his Special Forces unit in Al-Fallujah, Iraq. We gave him the serum and within hours, his skin had healed itself. We were elated! Our joy didn't last too long, I'm afraid."

"Why, Doc?" asked Franklin. "Did he die too?"

"No. His skin not only healed itself, but it also kept growing and growing. The military came in one day and removed him. I quit after that."

"So how does this explain what happened to me, Doc? Why am I jumping in time?"

"Better question," interjected Brooklyn, "why is he dragging me along for the ride?"

"That is something I have been thinking about since we met."

Dr. Classon began to pace and mumble incoherently to himself. Franklin and Brooklyn watched him for a few moments, their heads moving back and forth, like they were at a tennis match. He finally stopped pacing and stared at them intensely.

"This has the Director written all over it."

"The Director?" asked Franklin.

"When my team and I first started our research, we were able to change the cells of the blood sample we had. Problem was, we couldn't replicate it with any other samples. Then one day, a woman arrived in our lab. She had an amazing sample of blood! It was perfect, the ultimate vehicle. We were able to regenerate the cells and it became the basis for our serum."

"Who was this woman?" asked Brooklyn.

"She was known simply as The Director. We never got a real name."

97

"So why do you think she has something to do with it?"

"Because she was behind the military getting involved. I remember her pitch. 'This is a revolutionary breakthrough, gentleman. Enhanced soldiers. Particle manipulation. Advanced healing. We are scratching the foundations of life itself. If we can manipulate living matter to such a degree, it will only be a matter of time before we can manipulate the very essence of the origins of the universe. Time and space can bend to our will."

"And that's when they took over the project?" asked Franklin.

Dr. Classon didn't respond. His mind immediately began to contemplate how the company had achieved time travel, and why Franklin had been given it.

"If they were to attack the decay..."

"Doc," called Brooklyn.

"No. That wouldn't work because of the..."

"Doc!" shouted Franklin.

"But then if they infused the nuclei wall with the..."

"Doc!" a frustrated Brooklyn yelled.

"No. Doesn't account for the..."

The two had had enough.

"DOC!!!" they screamed in unison.

Dr. Classon snapped out of the conversation he held with himself.

"Oh, right! So, I have no clue how they did it. I have been out of the company for almost three years. But I know who will!"

He ran to the desk with the computer. He entered in his password and began to type. Franklin walked up behind him.

"Who are you emailing?"

"We are going to need help, and I know just the person."

"Who?"

"Someone still inside the company."

"Someone?"

"My ex-wife. She still works for the company."

Suddenly, an alarm sounded. It was a loud, industrial horn. Red lights came on and gave the warehouse an off-putting glow. Dr. Classon swung his chair over to the two screens to his right. The screen displayed a live feed from the security cameras outside. It was two men, dressed in all black, military styled outfits. Their tactical movements and use of hand signals revealed their military training. Each man carried a rifle close to their face as they focused their sight through the reticle.

"They found us fast!"

"Who found us fast?"

"The guys that were chasing us earlier."

Brooklyn ran to join them at the computer. She peered over Franklin's shoulder and spotted the men outside. Dr. Classon quickly finished his email and hit send. He ran over to his bedroom area, grabbed the keys to the van that he had dropped on the nightstand, and ran back to the van.

"Get in!"

Brooklyn and Franklin ran to the van, but it was too late.

BOOM!

Smoke filled the warehouse. The men used explosives to rip a hole in the gate, then threw two smoke grenades into the warehouse.

CLINK! CLINK!

Dr. Classon started the van. Brooklyn sprinted to it and slung the door open as the smoke became thicker.

"Franklin! Get in!!"

Franklin froze when he saw thin, red lights from laser scopes as they danced in the smoke. One of the lights stopped square on his chest. He began to hyperventilate as the small, red dot danced on his shirt like a bug. One of the men walked briskly by the van's open door, his rifle pointed at Franklin. Brooklyn watched in horror as the man approached Franklin, the red dot on Franklin's chest intensifying with each step he drew closer. *Oh my God! Franklin!* She leapt from the van and ran towards the man.

"NOOOO!"

His back was to her, but he heard her approach. He swung around to confront her, but she was already on top of him. She came at him full speed and wrapped her arms around him in a football tackle.

VLOOMP!

They disappeared.

"BRROOOOOOOOK!"

CHAPTER 7
THE PERFECT VEHICLE

Where did she go?? One moment she was there, tackling the man that tried to shoot him; the next, they both were gone.

"BROOKLYN!"

How?? Where did she..... The sounds of grunts and bodies as they smashed against the metal siding of the van broke Franklin's concentration. When the two armed men entered the warehouse, Dr. Classon crept out of the van and hid on the opposite side of it to ambush one of them. He sprung out just as Brooklyn disappeared and was now locked in a struggle with the second man.

"Doc!! DOC!!"

"Little...*grunt*...busy...right...now...*grunt*...Franklin!"

"Brooklyn! She disappeared!"

"That's fascinating! *grunt grunt* But now isn't the time!"

Franklin ran over to the other side of the van. Dr. Classon and the other man wrestled against the van, each with their hands on the rifle. Franklin searched for something, anything to help him out. *Oh man! Oh man! What am I gonna...a stool!* He ran over to the computer desk, hastily grabbed one of the stools, then sprinted as fast as he could back to Dr. Classon.

"Little help here, please!" screamed Dr. Classon, noticeably out of breath.

PING!

Franklin cracked the armed man in the back of the head as hard as he could. The man fell straight to the floor. Franklin was in shock by what he just did. Dr. Classon was hunched over, his hands on his knees as he breathed heavily.

"Now..... **gasp**gasp** ...what were you... **gasp**gasp** ...saying about Brooklyn?"

"She just disappeared!"

BANG!

Brooklyn was disoriented and her vision was blurry. *What just happened? Where am I??!?* She felt slightly nauseous. *I feel like I did in the park!* As her eyes slowly regained focus, she realized she wasn't in the dark, smoke filled warehouse. She was on the pavement just outside of it. *How...how did I get outside?* She could see through the hole in the gate and saw the van. Then she heard Franklin scream.

"BRROOOOOOOOK!"

She was about to yell to him to let him know she was alright, then she saw the man she attacked to save him. He was on his back next to her, even more disoriented than she was. Though part of her brain was in a frenzy about how she and the man ended up outside, the other part of it wanted to stop the man once and for all. *I gotta get to him before he gets up!* She frantically stumbled to stand up, her hand low to the ground as she regained her balance and searched for something to subdue him.

Brooklyn scanned the ground for something to hit him with; something hard and heavy. The blast the two men caused to get into the building damaged the warehouse's brick walls and scattered rubble everywhere. She quickly ran over and picked up a damaged brick. The man labored to get up and his eyesight hadn't regained its full focus. His arm flailed in a side-to-side motion as his open palm hit the concrete sidewalk in search for his rifle just a few feet away from him.

Brooklyn saw he had almost located his gun. Though still on his knees and disoriented, the man sensed Brooklyn approach from his rear. His fingertips found the strap to his rifle. He yanked it to him, found the grip, placed his finger in the trigger, then swung around and pointed the gun in Brooklyn's direction. She ran over to him just as he picked up the rifle. *No, you don't!* She gave a swift kick to the muzzle of the gun, sending it skyward as he fired a shot.

BANG!

Still a bit dazed, the momentum of her kick caused the man to fall back. Brooklyn quickly straddled him, then hit him with the brick square across the face. His head snapped to the side as blood sprayed from his mouth and onto the pavement. She sat on his chest, cocked the brick back behind her head, and hit him in the temple with one swift blow. As Brooklyn remained straddled over the unconscious man, Franklin, and a completely winded Dr. Classon emerged through the hole in the gate. Franklin ran to her.

"Brook!"

She turned around to see him run to her and opened her arms to embrace him. She didn't care that he had just called her "Brook." She only cared that he was unharmed. He threw his arms around her. Brooklyn had

105

never felt him hug her so tightly, but it reminded her of earlier that morning in his room. She dropped the brick and hugged him back. Franklin looked down at the man's bloodied face.

"What happened? I thought I'd lost you again!"

"I don't know. One second, I was in there and saw that man about to shoot you. The next, I was out here."

Franklin leaned back and the two stared at each other in amazement.

"Ummmm, can we go before these two wake up?" a concerned Dr. Classon asked.

Franklin and Brooklyn turned from looking at Dr. Classon, locked eyes, and nodded in agreement. Dr. Classon went back through the hole and into the warehouse. He hit a button and a door at the far end of the warehouse began to open. The siblings were startled by the noise, but knew it meant there was another way out other than the damaged gate they entered through. As they started to join Dr. Classon in the van, Franklin stopped, doubled back, and grabbed the rifle from the man that Brooklyn knocked out.

"A gun, Franklin?"

He shrugged his shoulders.

"Never know if we might need it."

HONK! HONK!

"We need to go!" commanded Dr. Classon.

The siblings ran into the warehouse, climbed into the van, and Dr. Classon pulled off as Franklin slid the van door closed behind them. He drove past his mini laboratory, swung a left, then around the back of the computers. The other side of the warehouse was dark, but light poured in at the far end of the building as the alternate gate opened. The van's tires screeched as he slammed the brakes and made a hard left out of the door.

"Ok," started Dr. Classon, "what happened back there?"

"I don't know," explained Brooklyn. "I just somehow got outside."

"What do you mean you 'got outside'?"

"I mean I tackled the man that was gonna shoot Franklin and then we were outside."

"You mean you teleported?"

"I guess. But how is that possible?"

"I don't know. I need to take you two somewhere to run some tests. Besides, I need to meet up with Tami."

"Who is Tami?" wondered Franklin.

"The person who is going to help us."

"And where are we going for these tests?"

"Oh! To my secret lab."

"Your secret lab?" remarked Brooklyn incredulously.

"If you had a secret lab, why didn't we go there first?" asked an astonished Franklin.

"Well, if I just take anyone there, it isn't much of a secret, now is it?"

Brooklyn threw her hands up and leaned back into her seat. Franklin shook his head in disbelief then dropped it into his hands. Dr. Classon turned to see them and was taken aback by their reactions.

"What?"

Franklin turned to Brooklyn. Her brow was wrinkled with worry and confusion.

"You okay?"

"No. What's happening to us?" she whispered.

"I don't know. Hopefully, Doc can get us some answers."

"You trust him?"

"He has saved us twice so far. Those men weren't trying to sell us cookies."

"I know but..."

"But what?"

"Don't you find it a little strange that he just happened to be at the park when we got back? Why does he know so much about this company and these men?"

Franklin watched Dr. Classon as he drove and barked commands at the van's onboard computer.

"Computer, send a distress email to Tami. Tell her to meet me at the place she said she would never set foot into."

Franklin leaned into Brooklyn but kept Dr. Classon in his sight.

"Yeah, I trust him. There's something familiar about him. Like, I've seen him before."

Brooklyn sighed.

"We need to get to Mom and Dad."

"And say what, Brook? I mean Brooklyn."

Brooklyn reached out and touched his leg, her non-verbal signal that calling her Brook was okay. He gave a slight smile before he continued.

"What would we say to them? They don't even know we exist."

Brooklyn fell silent. *Guess he's right. How would we explain to Mom and Dad they were their kids from the future...I think?* Then she looked at Franklin. *Why is he so calm? Why is he so different?*

"Franklin."

"Yeah?"

"You're different."

"What do you mean?"

"You're the confident one, the cocky one. You're the one that...I don't know. You seem so shaken, but crazy as it sounds, you're actually nice to me!"

109

I'm the cocky one??? I'm nice to her? Am I normally mean to her? He didn't know how to respond. How could he answer for a version of himself he had never met? Then a scary thought occurred to him, one that until that moment had never crossed his mind. *Wait! There are different versions of me?!?!*

Franklin was just as bewildered by the day's events as Brooklyn was. His train of thought was soon broken by Brooklyn's repeated pats on his leg with the back of her hand. He turned and immediately saw what she stared at out of the side window. He leaned across her to get a closer look.

"Where are we?"

They drove the rest of the way in silence. Dr. Classon had them in another desolate area. The van turned down back streets, alleyways, and quiet industrial roads, before finally slowing down in front of an old chemical plant. The building was abandoned and surrounded by a rusted chain link fence that was less than structurally sound.

A sign that read "UNDER TWENTY-FOUR HOUR SURVEILLANCE" was mounted against a gate that had wheels at the bottom. The pavement had random weeds that grew tall between the cracked asphalt. The windows were painted over and there was an odd smell in the air that filled the van. There were large, metal drums, stacks of damaged pallets, loose pipes and chains scattered about the grounds.

Dr. Classon eased into the brakes as he got to the rolling gate. He rolled his window down and leaned out to punch in the access code on a metal box. The mechanical motor that controlled the gate engaged and the gate slowly rolled open. They entered the property and Dr. Classon drove around to the back of the chemical plant. They finally came to rest in front of a loading dock. He turned the engine off, then exited the van.

"Last stop."

Brooklyn and Franklin exited the van and saw they were on a large, metal plate, large enough to fit the van. Dr. Classon jumped onto the four-foot raised, cement loading dock. Suspended from the awning on the dock was a yellow box attached to a long, thick black cord. As Franklin and Brooklyn made overtures to join him on the loading dock, he stopped them.

"No, stay right there."

Dr. Classon reached up, grasped the yellow box, and hit the two buttons in a rapid succession of presses and clicks. Suddenly, the metal plate began to lower into the ground. Franklin and Brooklyn were surprised as they realized the plate was an elevator. Dr. Classon quickly let the yellow box go and jumped off the loading dock and onto the plate. Franklin was impressed.

"You are full of gadgets, aren't you?"

Dr. Classon grinned.

"Wouldn't be much of a scientist if I wasn't."

The elevator slowly made its way down a dark elevator shaft. Franklin watched the daylight above grow smaller and fainter the more the elevator lowered. A door finally slid over the opening. They were in complete darkness. Brooklyn searched for Franklin's hand in the darkness and grabbed his wrist before sliding down to his hand. She gripped it tightly. Franklin had a flashback to his dream in the hospital. *The little girl... The hand feeling for me in the darkness... Was that a dream? Or was I seeing the future?*

The elevator descended almost five stories then stopped suddenly. Dr. Classon stepped off the elevator and spoke.

"Computer, I'm home."

The lights flickered on until fully bright, revealing the complexity of Dr. Classon's lab.

"Whooooaaaaaaa," they exclaimed.

Instantaneously, the sounds of generators hummed, and large computer servers began to make

112

noise as they awoke from their dormant state. There were gigantic computer screens mounted to the walls which made the lab appear more like space command central than some underground hidden laboratory. There was a large apparatus that looked like it shot a laser beam, state-of-the-art computer stations, and even more laboratory equipment than the warehouse.

"Welcome home, Dr. Classon."

The computerized voice echoed throughout the laboratory. Dr. Classon strolled through the lab as casually as one might walk through the supermarket. Franklin and Brooklyn slowly walked in awe.

"What is all this?" inquired Franklin.

"This is my pride and joy. The company paid well; I mean *really* well. I was pretty high up the old totem pole before I left. Made quite a bit of money. While everyone else spent their fortunes on fancy cars, trips, and toys, I bought this. Nerds don't get to be popular very often, so when they have the chance to flaunt, oh boy, do they flaunt."

"What's the real reason you left, Dr. Classon?" a skeptical Franklin asked. Dr. Classon sighed.

"Truth is, I was forced out. I knew what we were doing was wrong, it was dangerous. I couldn't let it fall into the wrong hands. My team and I wanted to stop. Neither the company nor the military would allow it. They threatened us. When we all continued to refuse their demands, my team slowly started disappearing. Officially, they were transferred to one of our other facilities. Unofficially? I think they were killed."

"Why did they let you live?" asked Franklin.

"Because of what I knew. I was the only one that knew how to create the original formula. Well, me and one other scientist, but he had a bit of protection himself."

"Protection?" asked Franklin.

"What do you know about genetics?"

Franklin and Brooklyn turned their faces up in confusion. Then they glanced at each other, then back at Dr. Franklin and shrugged.

"Are you two hungry?"

Before either could respond, Dr. Classon gave another command.

"Computer, prepare three dinners please?"

"Very well."

Dr. Classon turned to them both.

"How do I explain this?" he asked himself as he gazed up at the ceiling. "The human genome is a spectacular creation. Each genome provides specific details for how an organism will grow, its strengths and weaknesses, its height, gender, among other things. It also can reveal potential diseases and deformities. When The Director arrived with the baseline blood sample, my team and I analyzed it and discovered this specific sample was perfect, but in ways we had never seen before."

"Perfect?" asked Brooklyn.

"Yes. No deficiencies. No weaknesses. It was strong, withstood extreme heat and cold. It was amazing, but it wasn't from our world."

114

"Not from our world?" asked a confused Franklin. "You're saying it was alien blood?"

"No. It was human, but it had evolved. Our cells have twenty-three pairs of chromosomes, forty-six chromosomes in total. Each chromosome carries specific information and makes up DNA, and basically determines what a specific cell is supposed to do."

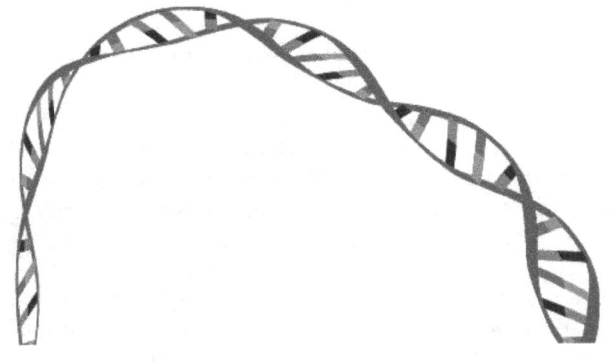

"We learned about that in biology," Brooklyn exclaimed. "How they were mapping all the genomes and could one day find the basis for life itself."

"Yes," affirmed Dr. Classon. "We are nowhere close to mapping the full human genome, but we have a basic idea of what we should see. That was until that blood sample. This sequence had twenty-four pairs and seven unique gene sequences we had never seen before. It was remarkable! We theorized that this type of evolution or gene mutation could take millennia to even appear, let alone evolve to a point of producing useable traits."

"So where did it come from?" Brooklyn asked.

"None of us said it, but we all thought it: the future. But the cell structure of this sample was genius in its simplicity and beauty. At its core, it rebuilt blood cells into pretty much whatever you wanted it to. Not only that, but it also replicated at a surprising rate so damaged or dying cells would quickly be regenerated or replaced. Its why it made it the perfect vehicle to deliver nutrients. But what The Director wanted was to use its unique properties to enhance people, change their DNA at a fundamental level."

Franklin's face turned up.

"What makes you think she got it from the future?"

"The Director never told us where she obtained it. She never told us anything about herself and we couldn't find anything on her. Her problem was replicating the cells to pass on its special properties without severely damaging or killing the new host, and therein lies my advantage. They can't recreate it, not without me. I figured it out and now I am the only one that knows the exact sequence the proteins must be synthesized in for it to remain stable. So, in exchange for my life, I promised to remain silent about what I knew, but only if I made one final batch. Enough to keep them busy for a while."

"Well, if you knew it was wrong, why did you do it?" asked Brooklyn.

"Tami."

"Who?"

"His wife, Brook. Tami is his wife. They threatened her, didn't they?"

Dr. Classon slumped down into one of the many computer chairs throughout the laboratory. His face was riddled with heartbreak and concern.

"First, they ruined me. They planted large sums of untraceable money in my accounts. Then, they made it seem like I had an affair and leaked just enough evidence to Tami for her to believe it."

Brooklyn folded her arms and frowned at him with contempt.

"I didn't! I would never! Tami was...Tami *is* my everything!"

Franklin gave Brooklyn a nudge. *She is always so skeptical!*

"After she left me, they forced me out under threat of prosecution for espionage, using the untraceable deposits as leverage. I had already bought this place, so I decided to accept their proposal and conduct my own research. Then I got a video in an email. It was just videos of her; at the mall, at the park, entering church, even getting ready for bed. The voiceover told me that they would be watching both the legal and illegal markets for the compounds needed to produce the serum. If they saw any combination of those compounds moving, for any reason, the next video I received wouldn't be so friendly."

With that, he dropped his head in his hands and began to openly cry. Brooklyn felt bad for how harshly she had judged him. Franklin walked over and put his arm around him. He knows how Brooklyn's wrath can feel.

"Well, there is one market they won't be able to trace, Doc."

"What do you mean?"

Franklin stuck his arm straight out in front of him, slid his jacket sleeve up and exposed his veins.

"Think you can get it out of there, fix this and send us home?"

Brooklyn walked over to him and made the same gesture. Dr. Classon smiled at them.

"That's a great start, but there are a few things we'll need that I don't have here."

"So, how do we get it?"

BUZZZZZZZ! BUZZZZZZZ! BUZZZZZZZ!

Dr. Classon swung around to the computer station where he sat and began to feverishly type. A window popped up on the screen that showed the security feed from the loading dock. It was a very beautiful woman. She impatiently stared into a security camera overhead that she obviously knew was there.

"You called me here, Monroe. Now let me in!"

Dr. Classon smiled. Tami got his email.

CHAPTER 8
SHOCK AND AWE

Brooklyn and Franklin were expecting the woman to use the elevator they rode down on. Dr. Classon reached over and pressed a blue button. The metal platform the van was parked on began to rise. When the woman heard the elevator begin to ascend the shaft, she was quick to correct Dr. Classon's false assumption.

"Monroe, I am not riding the service elevator. Open the door and I'll take the stairs."

He leaned into the microphone while he simultaneously pressed a button that unlocked the door to her left.

"Sorry."

They watched as the woman rolled her eyes and shook her head. She swung the metal door open and entered the building. Dr. Classon brought the elevator back down. Franklin stared down at Dr. Classon with one eye raised.

"She doesn't look too happy to be here, Doc," he noted.

"She hates this place. Hated it the moment I bought it. Said it was a waste of money, time and that I was too old to have a secret lair."

"Wellllll," started Brooklyn. "Now that you mention it."

"She has a point, Doc."

"It's not a secret lair! It's a hidden, highly advanced, completely secure...ok. It's a secret lair. But aren't you glad I have it?"

Franklin and Brooklyn both chuckled. Just then, a door to the far end of the room swung open behind them. They turned and saw Tami enter. She walked angrily yet purposefully towards them. They thought she was even more beautiful in person. She had brown skin the color of unrefined honey. Her dreadlocked hair was pulled back into a bun and highlighted her long neck adorned with pearls. She wore a dark blue pant suit with a white blouse and red high heels that echoed through the lair as she walked.

"Monroe, what is going on? And who are these children?"

Dr. Classon rose from his chair and approached Tami to intercept her.

"Tami, I know this looks bad."

"Looks bad? You email me, telling me you have an emergency and to meet you here. Then I hear about an explosion on the news near the old place! I swung by and there is a hole in the gate and cops all over! Then I come here, and you have kidnapped two children! So no, this isn't bad. It's a typical, crazy, Monroe Classon mess that I am *not* cleaning up!"

She rolled her eyes at Dr. Classon, leaned to the side, and studied Franklin and Brooklyn. Franklin and Brooklyn pensively returned the look. They were both startled by her reaction but understood why.

"I didn't kidnap them, Tami. They came here from the future, and I was just...."

"THE FUTURE? Oh, Monroe. Are you off your meds again?"

Franklin and Brooklyn were surprised by this revelation.

"You know I don't like those. They dull my senses. I thought they were a hallucination for a moment. When the men started chasing us though, I knew they were real. It was all real!"

"Men? What men?"

"You better sit down, Tami. You aren't going to believe this."

Tami came closer to where Franklin and Brooklyn were. She looked at them with a concerned, motherly look on her face.

"Hi, I am Brooklyn. I love your heels!"

"I'm Franklin...and Doc isn't crazy."

Their introductions caught her completely off guard. She slowly sat down, placed her purse on her lap, and the three frantically began to recount the day's adventure. Tami sat patiently, in disbelief by what she heard as Franklin, Brooklyn and Dr. Classon talked over each other in an excited manner.

"...so, I emailed you, that's when the men showed up and Brooklyn here discovered she can teleport! Teleport, Tami! The girl can jump through time and space!"

"Then we came here," Franklin stated, putting an end to the wild tale.

Tami stared at the three of them. She had so many questions, but only one mattered at this moment.

"Are you two on meds as well?"

"She doesn't believe us," Brooklyn resigned.

"Would you?" asked Franklin.

"Show her, Brooklyn," commanded Dr. Classon.

"Ummmm...I don't know how."

"Sure, you do! Just do it!" he demanded as he cleared chairs out of her way. Tami sat silently.

"Do it, Brook," encouraged Franklin.

"Franklin, I don't even know what happened or how I did it. I just wanted to stop that man from shooting you."

"I think your powers are connected to your feelings," Dr. Classon interjected. "Franklin, you said the first time you jumped was because you wanted to go back and stop the accident, then again when you saved Brooklyn in the car. Brooklyn, you teleported when you were protecting Franklin. Somehow, the two of you activate your powers when you want to protect each other. At least I think that's how it's working."

"Enough!" shouted Tami. "I have sat here and listened to this nonsense about time jumping and teleporting, about men in all black with guns. And you know what I think? I think he has drawn you two into his madness and obsession with the company. You two

122

should leave here. Like, right now. My *ex*-husband is sick."

She then turned to Monroe and compassionately placed her hand on his face.

"Monroe, this is wrong. Let these children go and get some help. Please."

He grabbed her hand from his face and held it in front of him.

"I did get help. I called you."

She pulled her hand from his grasp and placed her purse over her shoulder.

"You're leaving me no choice, Monroe."

Tami stood up and began to walk away.

"Where are you going?" Dr. Classon shouted.

"Back to the office, but I'll be contacting the police to let them know you have these two children down here. Get some help, Monroe."

"You can't call the police, Tami! Please!! We are telling the truth!" implored Dr. Classon.

"If the police come here, we are never going to get home. They definitely won't believe us," Franklin said.

Brooklyn knew he was right. She didn't want the police involved. She didn't want Tami to go back to the company. *She might tell the wrong people, and they already have sent armed men after us. If they sent two men last time, they could send an army the next time. I have to stop her!*

VLOOMP!

Tami was only a few feet from the door when a bright flash stopped her in her tracks. Brooklyn appeared in front of her. Tami screamed and stumbled backwards as her purse fell to the floor.

"Believe us now?" Brooklyn matter-of-factly asked.

"How?......How did.....But you were just..."

124

"Amazing, isn't it?" excitedly Dr. Classon asked as he approached her.

Tami spun around to look at Dr. Classon.

"Monroe, what have you done?"

"No, Tami. I am not at the company anymore. *You* are. The real question is: what are *they* doing?"

Tami slowly brushed passed Dr. Classon, in a state of shock and walked back to the chair she sat in before. Dr. Classon picked her purse up off the floor and followed her, Brooklyn right behind him. Franklin grabbed the chair she sat in previously and wheeled it over to meet her and help her sit down. She looked up at Franklin.

"You're *really* from the future?"

Franklin shrugged. "That's what Doc thinks. But he thinks you can help us get back home."

"How is this possible, Monroe?"

"I am still trying to figure it out myself. I have a few theories, but I need your help."

"My help? How can I help? I am no longer on the serum development team. I work in archives now."

"Perfect! That means you have access to research notes, lab reports and trial results. We can start there. What else have they been working on?"

"Monroe, you know I can't do that."

"Tami, when I was forced out, they were working on another version of the serum. One that allowed the subject to displace electrons in any object, in essence magnetizing the particles, allowing them to be moved with magnetic influence."

"The blue serum," she confirmed before her hand covered her mouth.

"So, they finished it?"

Tami nodded.

"Compound number three. They call it Project Hover."

"Project Hover?" a curious Franklin asked.

"In theory," Tami replied, "if it worked, it would grant the subject the temporary ability to interfere with electronics, magnetize particles, pushing or pulling them at will without touching them. We thought it might even allow the subject to bend the magnetic fields in their proximity, giving them the ability to levitate."

"You mean..." an astonished Brooklyn declared.

"Yes. It would give them the ability to fly."

Franklin and Brooklyn turned to each other with huge smiles on their faces.

"You said compound number three. What were compounds numbers one and two?" asked Dr. Classon.

"Compound one is Project Watertight. It's the one that drove you out."

"The skin invulnerability."

Tami nodded, though she continued to struggle to comprehend everything that just happened.

"And compound number two?" asked Dr. Classon.

"Project Brawn. It enhances the molecular structure of the muscles, heightens the reflexes."

"I didn't know about that one," responded Dr. Classon as he rubbed the stubble on his chin.

"Wait a second," a stunned Brooklyn interjected. "Are you telling me that they have a potion that will let you fly, make you invulnerable and give you super strength?!"

They then all stared at Tami. She nodded.

"I have seen memos for others as well. Project Intel, Project Tempo and Project Amalgam." She then turned to Dr. Classon. "Monroe, I swear I didn't know."

She bent over, collapsed her head into his knees and covered her face with her hands. Dr. Classon wrapped his arms around her to comfort her.

"They have been busy."

"How could I have been so blind? So stupid?!"

"It's not your fault."

"No, I mean about you...about us. That's why they forced you out. That's why they made everyone think you were crazy. You knew! I didn't believe you. *I'm soooo sorry, Monroe.*"

Tami began to sob. Franklin felt sympathy for Dr. Classon. *Having everyone, including the person you loved the most, think that you are crazy must be lonely.* Tami sat back up in the chair, her face awash with rage.

"We *have* to stop this!"

"We need to do some research first. Tami, I need a sample of whatever you can get your hands on. You have to go back."

"I can't go back in there. Not anymore."

"You have to. If we are going to bring the company down, I need as much data as you can get your hands on. Memos, notes, samples. Especially samples. Do you think you can get that?"

Tami nodded as she wiped her tears.

"Okay. I'll see what I can do. What are you going to do?"

"I am going to get some blood samples from Franklin and Brooklyn and run some tests."

"And what do we do while you two are playing spy and mad scientist?" asked Brooklyn, her arms folded.

Dr. Classon smiled at them.

"Practice. Let's find out exactly what you two can do."

CHAPTER 9
KEEP YOUR COOL

Tami left the lab, climbed the stairs, and walked to her car. She had no idea how she was going to get a sample of any serum without drawing suspicion. As she started the car, a wave of anxiety took over her body. She was still rattled by the story she had just heard and the confirmation with Brooklyn's display of her power. She was devastated now that she knew the home that she and Dr. Classon once shared had been attacked. But nothing shook her more than the knowledge that she abandoned Monroe.

It was too much for her to hold in. She began to hyper-ventilate. *Calm down, Tamala! You can do this!* She slowly pulled away from the chemical plant, approached the rolling gate, entered the code Dr. Classon gave her to come and go as she pleased, then started her mission.

"Maybe some music would help," she said aloud as she reached for the car radio to turn it on.

The radio station was no comfort, however.

Disc Jockey: *"Hey, friends. Now you know normally we are all about our smooth R&B, but I had to break in and kick it over to our news reporter, Cheryl Dawkins, on the scene of an apparent explosion. Cheryl."*

Reporter Dawkins: *"Thanks, Karl. In a developing story, an explosion happened earlier this morning at the warehouse district in downtown. Police are labelling this as an act of vandalism but have not ruled out terrorism. Reports indicate that the building is owned by a Doctor Monroe Classon, a former research scientist at..."*

Tami quickly changed the station and tuned to the first station that had music. It was the local country and western station. She wasn't particularly fond of country and western music, but any music would serve as a welcomed distraction and allow her to clear her mind.

♫ I'll be awaaaayyyyy,
But I'll be near your heart.

♫ Dontchu cryyyyyyyyy,
Please baby, don't you start.

♫ I'll be awaaaayyyyy,
But I'll be near your heart

"That's it!" she exclaimed.

Tami remembered that there was a small, off-site location close to the company's main headquarters. It was kept *away* from the main site for what she was told were security protocols. She knew that site not only had archives of past research, but samples of current batches of all projects were kept there. She could use her credentials as an archivist to get into the building. How she would get access to the samples was something she would figure out when she got there. With a smile and a renewed sense of confidence, she switched the radio off and sped up towards the off-site location.

"Might have to start listening to country music a little more often!"

Back in the lab, Franklin sat in a chair, his arm on the table and his sleeve rolled up. Dr. Classon walked over to him with a needle attached to a syringe, some test tubes for sample collection, alcohol swabs and bandages. He sat down on a stool and laid out the medical equipment.

"You ready, Franklin?"

VLOOMP! VLOOMP!

Franklin enviously looked past Dr. Classon and saw Brooklyn teleporting to different spots in the lab. *I am never gonna hear the end of how she can use hers, but I have zero idea how I use mine!* Dr. Classon cleaned off Franklin's arm and slowly inserted the needle.

"Ahhhhhhhh..." Franklin cried out as he winced.

Dr. Classon inserted one of the tubes into the back side of the syringe and the blood began to squirt, then flow smoothly to fill the tube up. Dr. Classon swung around on the stool and smiled at Brooklyn's growing proficiency with her ability.

"Brooklyn, what are you thinking about when you jump like that?"

"I realized you were right. It was my need to protect Franklin that triggered it. Then when Tami was about to leave, it was about protecting all of us. Then I tried to remember what I thought about right before I jumped. In the warehouse, I thought about wishing they never came in and they were still outside. With Tami, I thought about being in front of her and stopping her from leaving. But in both instances, I saw it in my mind."

"So, you have to see it in your mind to jump there. Interesting," he remarked as he rubbed his chin stubble again.

131

"Doc, think this one is full."

VLOOMP! VLOOMP!

"Oh! Sorry about that," he replied as he spun back around.

He removed the needle, cleaned the entry point again, then placed a bandage on Franklin's arm.

"Brooklyn, can you try something for me?" asked Dr. Classon.

VLOOMP!

She appeared right in front of him.

"Sweet Christmas!" Dr. Classon screamed.

"What's up, Doc?" she asked with an excited smile.

"First off, never do that again!" he scolded as he held his chest, scared from fright. "Try jumping someplace you have never seen before."

"Like where?"

"Have you ever seen where the Borneo tribes of East Kalimantan live?"

"The who of what where?"

"The Borneo tribes. Try and leap there."

"Ummmm....yeah, okay."

Brooklyn closed her eyes and concentrated. Nothing happened.

"Ooookaaaayyyyy. Let me try that again."

This time she shut her eyes tightly and balled her hands into fists. She strained so hard Franklin and Dr. Classon could see the veins in her neck begin to bulge. Again, nothing happened. Dr. Classon stood up, walked over to a computer, and began to type. The clicking of the keyboard strokes broke Brooklyn's concentration. She opened her eyes and saw Franklin's eyes closed and his hands balled into fists. He shook his body in a silly manner, an exaggeration of her trembling as she attempted to leap to a destination unknown.

"Really, Franklin?"

He burst out into laughter.

"At least I know how to use my power, punk!"

This made Franklin quickly quiet down.

"Here, Brooklyn. Look at this picture."

Franklin and Brooklyn walked over to the computer and looked over his shoulder. There was a picture of a tribal man adorned in colorful, ceremonial garb, standing in a clearing. She noticed the shades of bright orange, red, and blue of the beads that covered the man's chest plate and headdress. He had a thick, black beard and some sort of tribal weapon in his hand.

"You want me to leap to him?"

"No. I want you to leap to the spot in this picture where he is standing. Look at the trees, the slope of the hill behind him. Concentrate on the gravel on the ground. I want you to *see* the place he is standing, not him."

133

Brooklyn studied the photo. She began to see the deep blue of the sky, the height of the trees and their relative distance to the clearing the man stood on in her mind. She imagined herself standing where he stood.

"Now, Brooklyn. Keep in mind there is a twelve hour..."

VLOOMP!

"..time difference between here and...."

VLOOMP!

"..there."

"OH MY GOD, DOC! Its pitch black there and I am certain I heard a bear! Why didn't you tell me it was the middle of the night there??"

"I was trying to but...never mind. So, we have established that you must see or have previously seen where you are leaping. If you've never seen the place, you can't leap there. That's why you were able to do it at the warehouse and again here."

"That's pretty cool, Brook," an impressed Franklin said.

"Sit down and rest. Besides, I need to draw some of your blood. Franklin, your ability is a bit trickier than Brooklyn's. My hypothesis is Brooklyn is jumping in space, using time as a tunnel if you will. You seem to use space as a tunnel to jump in time. So, with you, we must be careful. Wouldn't want you jumping to the Jurassic period by accident."

"Dinosaurs! That would be kinda cool," Franklin approvingly responded.

134

"You'd get eaten by a T-rex the moment you arrived, idiot," Brooklyn retorted.

"She's kinda got a point there, Franklin, even if her bedside manner was a little harsh. We need to start small, manageable leaps over seconds and not huge ones over years. Let's try this," Dr. Classon explained as he slowly inserted the needle into Brooklyn's arm.

Brooklyn saw the needle go into her arm, but when the blood began to flow, she became lightheaded and passed out. Dr. Classon jerked his head back in surprise.

"Wasn't expecting that to happen. Anyway, Franklin, I want you to concentrate on my words. I am going to say the alphabet. When I get to letter G, try to jump back to when I began at A. Okay?"

"I'll try."

"I want you to concentrate on me saying the letter A. That is where you want to be. Not in that place, but in that moment. Got it?"

"Got it."

"Let's start. A...B...C..."

As Dr. Classon began to recite the alphabet, Franklin concentrated on the moment he was instructed to. *Go back to the A. Go back a few seconds to the A.*

"D...E..."

Then, something happened that shocked him. He didn't jump back in time, time slowed down. He wasn't going back in time, he moved slowly through it. He looked over at Dr. Classon and watched his mouth move.

"Eeeeeeeeeeffffffffff.....Geeeeeeeeeeeeeee."

He even heard him speak in slow motion. He then focused on Brooklyn. She was still passed out but the syringe in her arm told its tale. The blood flowed from her veins and into the test tube slowly like thick molasses in the winter.

"Whooooaaaaaaa! You guys are moving in super-slow motion."

His excitement broke his concentration. Dr. Classon gawked at him strangely, as if he were from another planet.

"What did you just say, Franklin?" asked a puzzled Dr. Classon.

"I just said you were moving in super-slow motion. What did you hear?"

"An indecipherable sound."

"And the blood in the syringe, it moved super-slow," Franklin added.

"By slow, do you mean you were moving fast?" inquired Dr. Classon, truly intrigued by this discovery.

"No, I never moved. Everything just started going slow."

Dr. Classon removed the needle from Brooklyn's arm, then cleaned and dressed her entry wound just as he did for Franklin before her. He stood up and walked away from her, passing Franklin as he did. He never took his eyes off Franklin as he walked by. Brooklyn began to regain consciousness.

"What did I miss?"

Before Franklin could tell her that he figured out part of his powers, Dr. Classon had reached the other side of the lab.

"Franklin, I want you to try to do that again for me on my mark, okay?"

Dr. Classon opened a drawer in a desk about fifteen feet away from where Franklin stood, reached in, and pulled out something that he hid behind his back. Brooklyn stood up slowly and stumbled a bit.

"Sure, Doc. What's the mark?"

"This! Brooklyn!"

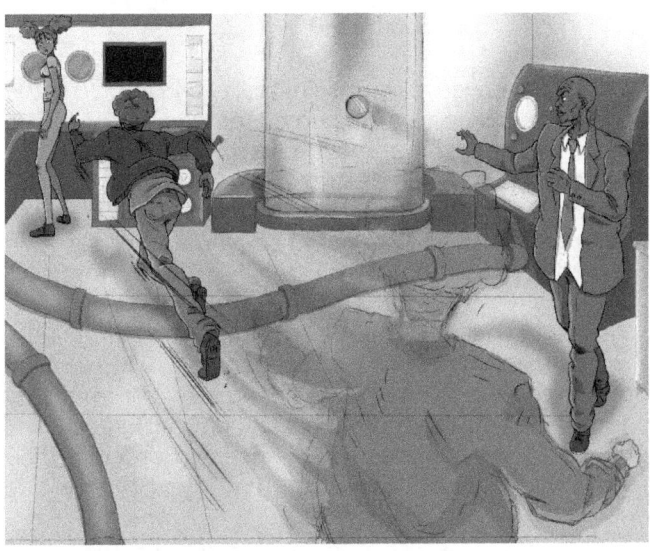

When he called her name, he pulled his hand from behind his back to reveal a tennis ball, which he threw at

Brooklyn.   Brooklyn, half-asleep, recoiled.   Franklin engaged his ability and marveled as the tennis ball slowly sailed through the air. He looked over at Brooklyn and saw her slowly continue to recoil in anticipation of being struck with the ball. He ran closer to her, got right in her face, then burst into laughter at the sight of her face all scrunched up.

Franklin laughed for what seemed like an eternity, but the tennis ball had barely moved twelve inches. Then he smiled and freed his mind. Time resumed at normal speed. The tennis ball struck Brooklyn's thigh with a soft thud.

"OW! What the heck, Doc?"

Franklin smiled bigger than he had ever in his life.

"I can slow down time!"

Tami arrived at the off-site facility and parked in the large, open parking lot. She noted there were only a few cars there, something she expected as the crew that manned the small, non-descript building had always been kept to a minimum. The facility was hidden in plain sight, underneath a small pharmacy. She exited her car then proceeded to the front door.

Tami knew the drill: walk in, go to the counter, ask the pharmacist to refill a prescription you called in for a patient, and when he asks if you would like it in twenty milligrams or fifty milligrams, answer fifty milligrams. The pharmacist will say that he will need to order it, then reach underneath the counter and buzz you into the side door.

All archivists were trained on the protocols to enter a storage facility. Though she was one of the leads on the archival team located at headquarters, and her name was known amongst all archivists throughout the company, protocols had to be followed. Her title would curry no favor. *Get it together, girl.* She took a deep breath and entered the pharmacy.

The pharmacy was empty, save for a cashier that tended to an elderly woman with her purchases, an armed security guard at the door, and the pharmacist in the back. The pharmacy had three aisles, lined with the typical fare one would see in a pharmacy. She smiled and nodded at the tall, muscular security guard as she entered. He returned the gesture. She walked down the first aisle full of cough remedies, pain relievers, band-aids, bandages, antiseptic ointments, and sprays. She approached the pharmacist who set the newspaper he read down to greet her.

"Hello. How can I help you?"

"Hi. I need to refill a prescription I called in for one of my patients."

"How would you like that to be filled? Twenty milligrams or fifty milligrams?"

"Twenty milligrams, please."

The pharmacist became skeptical. She realized her mistake and became nervous. *Dang!*

"Did I say twenty? I meant fifty. Fifty milligrams."

The pharmacist frowned and gave a suspicious glare.

"It's been a long day," she offered, a poor attempt to appear as if the mistake was no big deal.

"Do you have identification?"

This was not supposed to happen. He was simply supposed to buzz her in. She had to appear unphased. *Stay calm, Tami. Just show him your company ID. Don't seem nervous. Keep your cool.* She nervously smiled and nodded, then fumbled through her purse. The pharmacist subtly spied past her and locked eyes with the security guard at the door. The security guard noticed the look on the pharmacist's face, nodded, and slowly started to approach her from behind.

As he walked down the aisle Tami had travelled moments before, she saw him with her peripheral vision and became more nervous. Her hand began to shake in her purse. *Where's that ID!?* Finally, she found it. She produced the company ID, just as the security guard arrived two feet behind her. She nervously shoved it at the pharmacist. The pharmacist accepted the ID from her, examined the picture on the small, plastic card, then slowly returned it to her.

"No problem, Dr. Classon."

He reached under the counter and pressed a button.

BUUUUZZZZZZZZZZZZZ!
CLICK!

The buzzing sound and subsequent click startled her. The security guard peered down at her from behind. As the pharmacist handed her ID card back to her, she checked on the security guard with her peripheral vision. He hovered over her from behind. He was not smiling this time. She hastily stuffed her ID card back into her purse, walked away from the security guard and pharmacist, and through the secure door. When the door closed behind her, she leaned up against it, closed her eyes, and gave a sigh of relief.

"Whew!"

Tami took a few moments to calm down. *Breathe.* Her heart pounded within her chest. She opened her eyes to survey the room. It was a small, dimly lit room that measured no more than five by seven feet. The elevator had a unique keypad. Instead of a button to call for the elevator to go down, there was a small digital screen and a key card receptacle. She took her ID card back out of her purse and inserted it into the receptacle. After a few moments, the screen illuminated, and a digital version of her ID card was displayed on the screen. The outside of the pad lit up green and the elevator door opened.

She entered the elevator and pressed the only available button. It was labeled ARC, short for archive. The elevator door closed and descended to the archive below. Back in the pharmacy, the pharmacist and security guard still stood and their previous positions.

"Something is not right," observed the security guard.

"I'll make the call," responded the pharmacist.

CHAPTER 10
LET GO

The elevator reached the bottom floor and the door opened. When Tami entered the dark room, the motion sensor turned the lights on. The floor was made of thick, glass, illuminated from below by soft, fluorescent lighting, making the floor look like a smooth piece of ice. The archive was a series of computer servers, at least twenty by her count, and lined the walls to her left and right.

There was a single computer terminal at a small desk in the center of the room. In the back of the room was a small, crystal-clear box on a pedestal. Inside of the box were three vials, each containing a blue liquid. She recognized their contents instantly. *Project Hover! But where are the rest of the samples?!* She reached into her purse to get her cellphone. She sucked her teeth. *No bars! I'm too deep underground.*

Tami sat down at the desk and turned the computer monitor on. As the company logo slowly appeared on the screen, she searched her purse for her thumb drive. When she found it, she plugged it into the computer terminal and logged in using her executive level password. She hurriedly searched for any information she could find pertaining to Project Hover. As she opened file after file, her hand slowly began to cover her mouth, stunned by what she found.

"This isn't just the off-site back up for data on Project Hover. This is the main data back-up for all projects!"

She knew she had limited room on her thumb drive. *No time to reformat this drive. Just grab whatever you can, Tami.* She filled the thumb drive up with as much Project Hover data as she could, then used her cellphone to take pictures of other important documents. One was of particular interest. There were no names of people, only titles, but she knew who they all were.

March 18th, 2021

From: The Driver
To: The Director
Subj: Implementation of Phase Three

Ma'am, we have made significant advancements with Project Watertight, Project Brawn, Project Hover and Project Intel. Estimate deployable prototypes to be ready within six to nine months.

Project Tempo is in its infancy; however early test results reveal promising results. With these findings, we would like to begin Phase Three, with your permission, and move forward with Project Aspect. Our current timetable has us four years ahead of schedule in completing Project Amalgam.

Our team is standing by for further guidance.

Tami had only heard brief mention of Projects Amalgam, Tempo, and Intel, but had no knowledge of what each serum was supposed to do. The date on the document was of particular interest. *2021??? How is that even possible?? Who writes a memo for 10 years in the future??* Confused, she snapped a picture of the memo, then read the next document.

145

February 3rd, 2021

From: The Driver
To: The Director
Subj: Project Locations

CODE NAME	LOCATION
Project Watertight	2011
Project Brawn	1974
Project Hover	2015
Project Intel	2022
Project Tempo	2678
Project Aspect	2165
Project Amalgam	**CLASSIFIED**

This makes no sense! What do these numbers mean? She checked her watch and realized that she had been there for almost ten minutes. *This is going to draw suspicion if I am here much longer. I need to go!* She stood up, removed her thumb drive from the terminal, then powered it down.

She turned around and walked to the box holding the samples of Project Hover. She pressed the automatic release button on the side and the top slowly opened. There was a hiss as a rush of air broke the vacuum seal on the box. She grabbed all three vials, stuffed them, her cellphone, and the thumb drive into her purse, and then turned to leave.

She inserted her ID card and the elevator door opened. She smashed the button, but nothing happened. *The elevator can only be sent down from the* inside. It was then she noticed the phone. There were no numbers, only a solitary red button. She picked up the receiver and pressed the red button.

"All done, Dr. Classon?"

"Yes, I am. Can you bring me up please?"

"We seem to be having a bit of trouble with the elevator. Give me a second."

The pharmacist pulled the phone that connected to the elevator away from his left ear and placed a red phone receiver against his right.

"She is requesting to come up. What do you want me to do?"

A mechanically disguised voice on the other end of the line answered.

"Bring her up. Keep her there. We have two teams arriving shortly."

"Understood."

Tami became extremely scared. *This isn't good! What is taking so long? Do they know what I was doing?* She started to pace, then spotted the camera in the corner of the elevator. *They're watching you, girl! Stay. Calm. Tami.* Suddenly, the elevator door started to close. She had ideas of jumping out, not wanting to be trapped in the elevator. She thought better of it and decided to stay put.

When the elevator started to ascend, her stomach dropped, relieved that she was being brought up. *I might pull this off yet!* When the elevator stopped, and the door opened, she almost tripped as she exited she was so nervous. She knocked on the door and heard the buzz and mechanical click that unlocked the door. She burst through it in a panic.

"Thank you very much."

She turned down the aisle she had walked down earlier and headed towards the door.

"Dr. Classon. Can you hold up a minute? I need you to sign the log of what you took from the archive," shouted the pharmacist.

Tami didn't stop. She briskly made her way to the exit. The security guard moved in to intercept her. Her heart began to race even faster. She knew she couldn't overpower him. Her eyes darted around the aisle for something to defend herself with. She saw a can of anti-fungal foot spray on the shelf. When the guard was almost on top of her, she grabbed the can of anti-fungal spray, ripped the top off and sprayed him in his eyes.

"AAAAHHHHHHHHHGGGHHHH!"

He screamed in pain and stumbled backwards, then into one side of the aisle. Bandages and bottles of alcohol fell to the floor. She saw her opportunity to escape. She pushed passed the guard which knocked him into a seated position on the floor, and she ran out of the pharmacy.

As the click-clack sound of her heels echoed through the empty parking lot, she frantically searched for her car keys as she headed for her car. When she got to her car, the pharmacy door swung open, and the pharmacist ran after her. Though her hand trembled, she was able to press the unlock button on her car, quickly climb in, then locked the door behind her. The pharmacist arrived at her car and began to bang on her driver side window.

"Open the door, Dr. Classon!"

She started the car and began to drive off. Just then, the security guard emerged from the pharmacy, his eyes squinted, and his gun drawn. He fired twice at her car.

BANG! BANG!
SMASH!!!

The first bullet missed the car; the second one shattered her back windshield and sprayed broken glass throughout the car. She checked her rear view mirror and saw the pharmacist point in her direction and give instructions to someone in a black sedan that wasn't there moments ago. A second sedan zipped by the first one in hot pursuit of her. She was panicked and she could barely breathe.

"CALL MONROE!" she shouted at her car's voice-recognition software.

RIIIIIINNNGGGG!!
RIIIIIINNNGGGG!!

"Pick up, Monroe!!!!"

RIIIIIINNNGGGG!!
RIIIIIINNNGGGG!!

"PLEASE!"

"This is soooooo cool!" exclaimed Brooklyn as she leapt from spot to spot in the lab.

Franklin sat in the corner. *I wish I could talk to Dad. He would know what to do, but this isn't my dad. I can't just walk up to him and say "Hey, I am your son from the future, and, oh yeah, I have superpowers!" I know Doc wants to help but I miss my...wait! UNCLE JASON!! He believed me when I was telling him about the first accident. At least I think that version of Uncle Jason did. The version of Uncle Jason now would be younger. Maybe he will believe me again!*

Franklin leapt from his chair and started to run, then remembered he had superpowers. *Slow.* Everything slowed down. Next to Dr. Monroe, a small ball of light floated in air. As he drew closer, the ball of light began to take shape. It was Brooklyn. She had leapt from one spot and was now taking form in another.

"Whooooaaaaaaa! I can move faster than she can leap!"

He stood next to the spot where Brooklyn would soon be, then allowed time to resume at normal speed.

"Brook!"

"AAAAAAAAAAAAAAAAAAAAAAAAAAAAAA!!!"

Brooklyn jumped to her left and landed on Dr. Monroe. Franklin laughed uncontrollably.

"Where did you come from?" shouted Brooklyn.

Franklin pointed to the seat he sat in before.

"Over there."

"Fascinating!" Dr. Classon exclaimed.

"What's that? That he almost gave me a heart attack?" asked Brooklyn.

"That I moved so fast I arrived before she could materialize?"

"Well, yes. Those are both fascinating too, but I am talking about your genome strand, Brooklyn. You have six of those unidentified gene strands I told you about earlier."

"How is that possible? That nurse gave Franklin the serum, not me."

RIIIIIINNNGGGG!!
RIIIIIINNNGGGG!!

Dr. Classon reached for his cellphone.

RIIIIIINNNGGGG!!
RIIIIIINNNGGGG!!

It was Tami.

"Hey, hon. Did you..."

"MONROE! LISTEN! THEY ARE FOLLOWING ME! THEY SHOT AT ME, MONROE!"

"Oh my God!"

"What is it, Doc?"

"They found out about Tami!" he shouted at Franklin in a panic before returning to the call. "Where are you?"

"Ummmm....I am......."

One car sped up and pulled alongside of her. The passenger extended his arm out of the window. His gun was pointed directly at her.

"MONROE!"

She slammed her foot down on the accelerator.

BANG! BANG!

"Tami!" screamed Dr. Classon.

Tami was frantic. She swerved in and out of traffic, fearful she wouldn't make it back to the lab. The two cars sped up. One rammed her from behind.

BAM!

"OH MY GOD, MONROE! WHAT DO I DO?"

"How close are you?"

"What's going on?" asked a still shaken Brooklyn.

"People are chasing Tami!" Dr. Monroe informed her.

"Chasing her? Where is she?"

"We don't know."

Brooklyn snatched the phone out of his hand.

"Tami, this is Brooklyn. I need you to take a picture of the inside of your car."

"*WHAT?!?! A PICTURE??*"

"Listen to me. Take a picture of the seat next to you."

Dr. Classon understood what Brooklyn wanted to do and snatched the phone back.

"Honey, listen to me. Do what she is asking. Take a picture and send it to me."

"I don't understand how that will..."

"TAMALA MARIE CLASSON! DO IT!"

Tami pulled the phone from her ear and stared at it for a moment, then threw it down in the seat next to her.

"She hung up!" Dr. Classon angrily shouted.

"What are we going to do, Doc?" asked Franklin.

Brooklyn had another idea.

"Do you have any old pics of her on your phone? In the car maybe?"

"Hold on!" said Dr. Classon as he began to swipe the screen on his phone.

Tami made it onto the highway but was nowhere close to the lab. One car rode alongside of her on the passenger side. The driver continued to ram the car into hers to run her off the road. The other car was still behind her, its bumper wedged against her back fender. She was trapped. Just then, the passenger in the car next to her opened his car door and stood up on the floorboard. He leaned out and pointed his gun over the roof of the car.

153

BANG!
SMASH!

Glass from her front passenger window sprayed all over the inside of the car.

"Leave me alone!"

BANG! BANG!

"I knew I never should have gotten involved with his mess! If I make it out of this, I am going to kill you, Monroe Classon!"

VLOOMP!

"Tami!"

"AAAAAAAAAAAAAHHHHHHHHHHHHHH!"

Tami swerved hard and almost lost control of the car. Brooklyn covered her mouth to hide a quick giggle. *Now I know why Franklin laughed.*

"Calm down. It's me, Brooklyn. What am I sitting on?"

"How....How....."

Brooklyn reached underneath her butt and pulled Tami's phone out, gave Tami a disapproving glare and shook her head.

"Next time, take the picture."

Ahead of them, there was a traffic jam. The men in the car next to her saw Brooklyn appear in the car. The passenger stopped firing, got back into the car, and pulled out a communication radio.

"The girl just appeared in the car! Should we still ram them off the road?"

The mechanically disguised voice replied.

"No. We need her alive. Capture her. Kill the woman."

The driver in the car behind them also heard the command through his radio. He began to accelerate, his bumper pushed Tami and Brooklyn head on into a sure crash up ahead. Brooklyn knew they had little time. In ten seconds or less they would smash into the cars stopped in front of them.
"Where is the stuff?"

Nine seconds.

"In....in...It's in my purse on the floor."

Eight seconds.

Brooklyn found the purse, picked it up, and placed the cellphone inside of it.

Seven seconds.

She held the purse in her right hand.

Six seconds.

She grabbed Tami's forearm with her left hand.

Five seconds.

"Let go of the wheel."

Four seconds.

"What?

The car behind them accelerated. The driver next to them drew a weapon out and aimed for the front tire.

Three seconds.

"Let it go!"

"We are going to..."

Two seconds.

"LET GO!"

One second.

Tami let go.

VLOOMP!
CRASH!!!

CHAPTER 11
RISE OF HEROES

VLOOMP!

Tami fell to the ground in the lab and began to vomit.

"Tami!" a relieved Dr. Classon cried out.

He ran to her side and kneeled next to her on the floor, then placed his arm around her. Tami flung his arm off her and wiped her mouth.

"Don't! Don't touch me!"

"Tami, I am so sorry that happened to you!"

"Sorry? You're sorry?" she snapped as she gathered herself and rose to her feet. "Which part exactly are you sorry for, Monroe? Having me sneak into the company's secure facility, stealing classified documents and a top-secret formula? Or was it being chased by a huge security guard with a gun? Or maybe it was being shot at? Multiple times, I might add!"

Franklin and Brooklyn watched in disbelief as Tami unleashed her tirade.

"Oh, I know!" she continued. "You're sorry I was chased by two cars attempting to run me off the road. Is that it? And how can we forget the minor thing of having an entire human being magically appear next to me, then magically teleport me milliseconds before I crashed! So, tell me, Dr. Monroe Classon, what exactly are you sorry for?"

"Everything. Except the last part. Bet you're pretty happy Brooklyn appeared, right?"

Tami stared at him in disbelief.

"You say you love me. You say that I am your world. How could you put me in that position? I could have died!"

"And I would have too."

Her eyes welled up.

"Don't do that, Monroe!"

Her voice quivered as she turned and walked away. He chased after her and slung his arms around her from behind.

"I am so sorry, my love. I lost you once and I don't know what I would do if I lost you again. You're right, I never should have put you in that position. It was dangerous and reckless."

Franklin and Brooklyn watched the drama unfold. Tami broke his embrace and spun around to face him.

"Do you want to know the *real* reason I left you, Monroe? It wasn't another woman. I don't think I ever believed that. You? With another woman? No, there was something else you were cheating on me with, and we are standing in it."

"The lab? You left because of the lab?"

"Yes! The lab, the work, your need to always be the smartest, to figure everything out. You left me long before I ever left you."

Dr. Classon's heart broke. Tami's words pierced his heart. She turned away and sobbed. Dr. Classon placed his arms around her.

"There was never anything I loved more than you. I am sorry I made you think otherwise."

Franklin walked over to Brooklyn and leaned in to whisper in her ear.

"Why are grown-ups so dramatic?"

"Shut up, Franklin! They're in love."

"That's being in love, huh?"

"Aren't you in *loooooove* with Danielle?" she retorted with a giggle.

Franklin frowned and turned the side of his mouth up. Suddenly, the lab's lights switched from fluorescent white to bright red and the alarm began to sound.

EERRRRGGGHH! EERRRRGGGHH!
EERRRRGGGHH! EERRRRGGGHH!

"The proximity alarms!" exclaimed Dr. Classon, as he darted over to the computer terminal and began to feverishly type.

Tami, Franklin, and Brooklyn quickly joined him. Dr. Classon brought the outside security footage up. With a few more keystrokes, he transferred the feeds to the many large television screens on the wall in front of them. Each of the eight televisions were assigned to a different camera's live feed and covered every entry point to the chemical plant and the gate perimeter.

The rolling gate they used to access the chemical plant grounds had been mowed down by a black sedan. Tami noticed the damage on the front of it and quickly surmised that it was the same vehicle that rammed her car from behind.

"Monroe! That's them!"

Another black sedan flew over the downed gate, followed by a large, armored, black cargo truck that reminded Franklin of a SWAT vehicle. Franklin noticed Brooklyn had stopped looking at the sedans and truck as they breached the compound. She stared at the floor where she and Tami appeared a few minutes ago. She was focused on Tami's purse.

"Are you thinking of doing what I think you are?" he asked.

Brooklyn didn't respond. She kept staring at the purse. Franklin became worried. *Doc told us not everyone can take the serum. What if she takes it and it kills her or deforms her? This is a mistake! I gotta make her see reason!*

"Doc, you said Brooklyn had six of those genomes that you had never seen. How if she never got the serum?" he asked, his eyes affixed to Brooklyn.

"I really can't tell you. But she definitely has them. It's fascinating, really."

"But if she or I take another serum, it could kill us, right?"

"Yes!" shouted Tami. "Neither of you can inject yourselves with that stuff! It's dangerous!"

"Actually, Tami, I think they could..."

That was all the confirmation Brooklyn needed. Before Dr. Classon could finish his sentence, she disappeared.

VLOOMP!

Franklin slowed time down and raced over to the purse.

ZIP!

As he got close, a small ball of light began to materialize near the purse. It was Brooklyn, teleporting to the spot. He began to run faster and scooped the purse up before she had finished teleporting. When she fully materialized, she was stunned to see Franklin already there, the purse in hand as he searched for the serum.

"I hate when you do that."

"I know, but you can't take this serum, Brook. We don't know what it will do to you."

"You got it and you're fine! Besides, I already have powers and I never got *any* serums!"

"He's right, Brooklyn," Tami shouted as she ran over to them.

Brooklyn became agitated. She focused on the purse in Franklin's hand.

VLOOMP!

She materialized behind him, snatched the purse, then disappeared again.

VLOOMP!

Before he realized what had happened, Franklin saw his hands empty. *Dang it, Brooklyn!* He slowed time down and waited to see where she would materialize. *Where are you?* The ball of light began to form near the table where Dr. Classon drew their blood. *Gotcha!* He ran over and stood in front of the table, but this time, he didn't speed time back up. He waited and when she had fully materialized, he calmly reached into the purse and removed the vials. He turned and grabbed a syringe and ran to the farthest corner of the lab. Then he let time resume as normal.

VLOOMP!

Brooklyn dug through the purse but came up empty.

"FRANKLIN! WHERE ARE YOU??!?"

Franklin locked eyes with Brooklyn.

"I won't lose you again. If anyone is taking this, it's me!"

"No, Franklin!" screamed Tami.

"Weeeeeee dooooooooon'ttt knoooooowwwww..." began Dr. Classon.

Franklin stuck one of the vials containing the blue serum into a syringe, jammed the needle into his thigh, then pressed the plunger. The pain became unbearable.

"AAAAAAAAAAAAHHHHHH!"

162

The serum began to course through his body. As it entered his bloodstream, the burning sensation was ten times more intense than the green serum he was given in the hospital. He dropped to the floor and writhed in pain, a pain so great, he could no longer manipulate time to his will. Brooklyn became terrified when she saw Franklin go from upright with the vials in his hand to scream in pain on the floor in an instant.

VLOOMP!

"What did you do?!!"

Franklin screamed and convulsed, his arms straight as boards and veins bulged from his neck. Brooklyn placed her arm under his head and held his convulsing body.

"PLEASE, FRANKIE!"

Dr. Classon pushed himself away from the desk and sprinted to Franklin. Franklin's convulsions stopped and he lie motionless, his eyes rolled to the back of his head. Dr. Classon placed his pointer and middle finger on Franklin's neck to check for a pulse.

"He's alive, but barely."

Brooklyn began to hysterically cry.

"NO! NO! NOOOO!!!!"

Tami ran over to a cabinet stocked with medical supplies. She grabbed a syringe of adrenaline and the advanced medical kit, then ran to join Dr. Classon and Brooklyn.

"Is he going to be okay?" implored Brooklyn.

"I don't know," replied Dr. Classon as he removed the breathing bag from the kit and started pumping air into Franklin's lungs.

BOOM!

The lab shook, even though the explosion was five-stories above them. Tami looked back at the large monitors. Two of the monitors were blinded by thick, heavy, black smoke. Vehicles continued to arrive, and a dozen men filed out of the truck. All of them were heavily armed and were outfitted in heavy, bullet-proof protective gear.

"Monroe!" she shouted and pointed at the monitors.

"Computer, initiate defense protocols," he commanded.

"Is this a Level One, Level Two, Level Three..."

"LEVEL FIVE!"

"Initiating Level Five defense protocols."

Outside, the men in black began to surround the building. They moved tactically like a special operations unit, much like the two men that attacked them at the warehouse did. The computer raised three gun turrets on the roof. Its tracking system utilized an advanced, infrared capability to home in all subjects.

"Please identify friend or foe, Dr. Classon," asked the computer.

Dr. Classon continued to tend to Franklin.

"Neutralize all personnel with weapons."

"Engaging."

Gun fire rained down on the attackers. They scattered in retreat to duck for cover.

"Monroe! When did you get all of this? And why do you have it??" Tami asked, shocked by the amount of artillery the building was equipped with.

"Do you really want to know?"

Franklin struggled to open his eyes. His vision was blurred, and his head rang with pain.

"What happened?"

Brooklyn gently punched him in the arm, then hugged him.

"You scared me half to death! That's what happened!!"

"Franklin," Dr. Monroe started, "how do you feel?"

"Besides the headache, no different."

Franklin rose to his feet. *Okay, let's see if all of that was worth it.* He remembered that Tami told them Project Hover would give him the ability to fly. He jumped and quickly fell back to the ground. He jumped again and fell again. *Maybe if I get a running start.* He slowed down time.

ZIP!

He ran and jumped. Nothing. He turned to Tami. "You sure this is supposed to make me fly?" he asked in frustration.

"According to the research I've seen."

BOOM!
BOOM!

The building began to shake and rubble from the roof fell to the ground. The men had retrieved a rocket launcher from the truck and had destroyed two of the three gun turrets.

"Defense weapons at thirty-three, point three percent," the computer informed Dr. Classon.

"Activate outer defenses. Direct fire inward at targets."

"Activating."

A series of smaller weapons began revealing themselves. They rose from old, rusted sixty-gallon drums, dumpsters and large, metal shipping containers.

"Paranoid much?" Tami asked.

"When they ask how many guns I need, the answer is always *more*."

BOOM!
TAT TAT TAT TAT TAT TAT TAT TAT!!
TAT TAT TAT TAT TAT TAT TAT TAT!!
BOOM! BOOM!
TAT TAT TAT TAT TAT TAT TAT TAT!!

Amid the chaos, Brooklyn stared at the two remaining vials of Project Hover. *If Frankie can survive it, so can I!* She grabbed one of the two remaining vials and injected herself. She immediately fell to the floor in pain, just as Franklin did before her. With all the surrounding noise from gunfire and explosions overhead, Franklin didn't hear her scream out.

As the perimeter defenses shot at the men in black, and they responded by throwing grenades and firing rockets to disable them, Franklin decided enough was enough.

"I may not be able to fly, but I know I can move fast enough to stop them!"

ZIP!

Before Dr. Classon or Tami could object, Franklin was gone. He ran up the flights of stairs and stopped on the loading dock. Dr. Classon knew he couldn't stop him but didn't want Franklin to get hit by friendly fire. He disabled the defense system.

"Computer, cease fire."

"Are you sure you would like to..."

"CEASE FIRE!"

The last gun turret on the roof stopped firing, as did the guns of the perimeter defense system.

"Cease fire, complete."

Franklin stood on the loading dock. He was terrified as he scanned the parking lot. All the men were still in their cover positions. None of them fired. None of them moved. *Why aren't any of them moving? Are they afraid of me?* He wanted to go attack them. He knew he needed to do something. *There's so many of them! I'm gonna have to move faster than ever to disable them.* Then Franklin looked down at his chest. It was covered in tiny red dots. The men had him in their sights.

Dr. Classon and Tami stabilized Brooklyn's convulsions and breathing and now stared up at the monitors. Brooklyn slowly opened her eyes. *What...what happened?* She saw Dr. Classon and Tami over her. She saw them transfixed by the monitors. She curiously focused on the monitor closest to her and saw Franklin, alone. Dr. Classon and Tami hadn't realized that Brooklyn regained consciousness until she spoke.

"Oh, no you don't!" exclaimed Brooklyn.

They immediately turned to her in relief and surprise, then realized she saw her brother alone on the loading dock.

"Brooklyn, wait! You can't..."

VLOOMP!

Brooklyn appeared next to Franklin on the loading dock. All the men lowered their weapons, shocked by her instantaneous appearance. Dr. Classon and Tami watched the monitors in horror. Neither wanted anything to happen to the kids.

"What can we do, Monroe? We can't let them fight those men! They'll get killed!"

"Let's get the van up there!"

"Don't move!" one of the men shouted at Franklin and Brooklyn. "There is no way out of this! You have company property! Turn it over and no one needs to get hurt!"

Franklin looked at Brooklyn. Brooklyn stared at the men, her fists balled up, her breathing was heavy. He knew she had her game face on, the look she had before every one of her races. He smiled, then turned back to the armed men.

"Oh yeah?" he shouted back. "Come get us!"

Brooklyn gave her baby brother a menacing smile. "Shall we?"

Franklin stared at the armed men with a fury she had never seen.

"Yes. I think we shall."

VLOOMP!
ZIP!
She reappeared next to one of the men and kicked him in the groin. A split second later, Franklin appeared with a long, thin pipe he picked up off the ground as he raced over and cracked him in the head.

ZIP!

Before the man had time to fall, Franklin zipped over and hit another in the back. He arched his body and shouted in pain.

VLOOMP!

Brooklyn appeared and punched him in his throat. Brooklyn decided to get a weapon of her own.

VLOOMP!

She leapt to the loading dock, grabbed a chain off the ground and wrapped it around her fist.

VLOOMP!

She appeared next to another man with a gun and punched him in the face.

ZIP!

Franklin zipped over and hit him in the chest with a pole.

"Let's split up. This is going to take forever," Franklin suggested. Brooklyn nodded in agreement.

"I'll go left," she shouted.

VLOOMP!
ZIP!

ZIP!
VLOOMP!

Back in the lab, Tami watched in awe as the siblings made quick work of the men. Dr. Classon ran back and forth from the lab to the van. He loaded it with the samples he drew from Brooklyn and Franklin, laptops, some laboratory equipment, medical supplies, and a lock box full of cash. On one of his loading trips, he slowed down to see what transpired above them.

"Amazing!"

"Yes, it is! But we have to get them out of here and fast! They knew exactly where we were."

"Trying to figure that part out, too."

VLOOMP!

Another punch to the face!

VLOOMP!

A kick to the ribs, then a punch!

ZIP!

The pole cracks another man in the face!

ZIP!

Another shin meets the wrong end of hardened steel.

Franklin shifted to his right and saw Brooklyn subdue the last of the men. Then, his heart sank. One of the men they had disposed of earlier had recovered behind her. He knelt on one knee. His gun pointed directly at her back.

"BROOOOOKLYYYYN!!!"

Dr. Classon and Tami gasped.

"NOOOOOOOOOOOOOOOOO!" Dr. Classon screamed.

Franklin slowed time down and ran as fast as he could. Brooklyn's head began to move slowly as she turned towards the sound of Franklin's voice she heard a few milliseconds before. The muzzle of the man's gun flashed!

BAAAAAAAAAAAAANNNNNNNGGGGG!

It flashed again.

BAAAAAAAAAAAAANNNNNNNGGGGG!

Then again. And again. And again.

BAAAAAAAAAAAAANNNNNNNGGGGG!
BAAAAAAAAAAAAANNNNNNNGGGGG!
BAAAAAAAAAAAAANNNNNNNGGGGG!

He ran faster and faster. He could see the bullets as they headed towards her, but they moved faster than he could get there. He began to cry. He couldn't lose her again. Not again. Not now. Not like this. He was only a few feet from her, but the first bullet was only a few inches from ripping through her back. He reached out for her and screamed!

"BROOOOOKLYYYYN!!!"

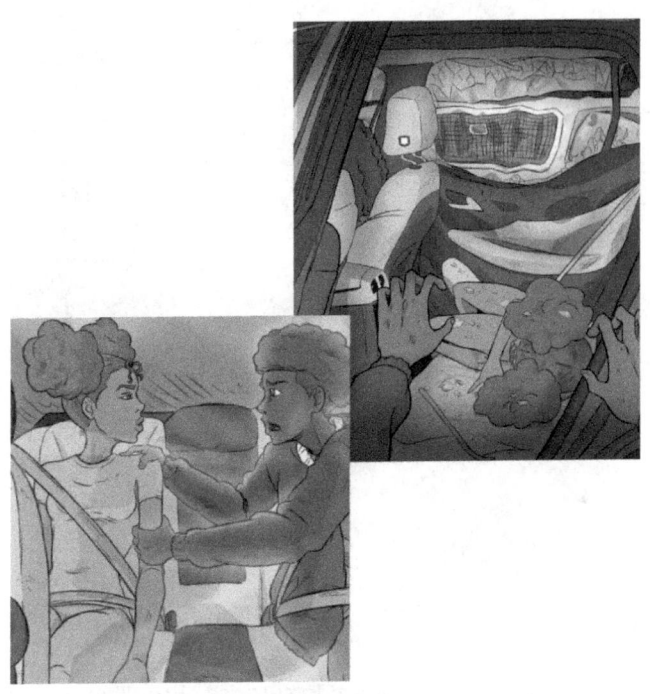

He was only two feet from her, but he couldn't save her. He saw the first accident. Him reaching into the van. He saw the second accident when he reached over and grabbed her and pulled her away from the impact of the truck. Now, no matter how hard he stretched or how fast he ran, he couldn't reach her.

Then, it happened. She began to fly away from him, rising off her feet, like she had been pushed.

Franklin slowed down in surprise. Brooklyn slowly floated up and away from him. He couldn't believe what his eyes told him. She slowly sailed backward and upwards into the sky. Franklin then watched in shock as the bullets flew past him through the space Brooklyn once stood. *What...? How...?* With his concentration broken, time resumed as normal.

YES!" screamed Tami, tears of relief and pure joy streamed down her face as she and Dr. Classon watched from below.

Though Franklin's intent was to reach out and grab her, somehow, he pushed her. Then he remembered what Tami told them earlier.

"...magnetize particles...pushing or pulling them at will without touching them...bend the magnetic fields in their proximity...ability to levitate..."

Project Hover didn't give him the power to levitate himself; it gave him the power to levitate objects! His love for his sister once again unleashed his power. The man that fired the gun now cowered, his eyes up at the sky. The men that weren't knocked unconscious, looked up as well, all of them shocked and amazed by what they saw. Franklin was the only one that had a smile on his face.

Brooklyn was disoriented. A second ago, she was punching a guy in the face with her chain-wrapped fist. Now her eyes darted around from fright as she saw the fallen men and her brother below. Her heartbeat fast and she could barely catch her breath. Franklin lowered his hand to bring her down. She was fifteen feet in the air, yet she stayed there. He was no longer the reason she was in the air.

Brooklyn could fly!

"Oh my god...." Dr. Classon cried out in an amazed whisper.

"How is she..." cried Tami.

Dr. Classon slumped down to catch his breath. He then gathered himself and ran to one of the computer servers. He removed one specific bank of the storage unit.

"System shut down in ninety seconds. Ninety. Eighty-nine. Eighty-eight. Eighty-seven..."

"We have to go," he commanded as he ran to the van. He placed the storage unit into the van and slammed the door. "Tami!"

She was jarred out of her frozen amazement and ran to the van. Dr. Classon walked over to a panel on the wall. He opened it and revealed a large lever that looked like an upside-down football goalpost. He threw the switch, and the elevator began to rise.

"Sixty-four. Sixty-three. Sixty-two..."

He ran to the elevator lift, jumped on, then climbed into the van as the elevator rose to the roof and into the elevator shaft.

Brooklyn stared down at Franklin.

"You saved me."

He smiled.

"You needed saving. Again."

She smiled and rolled her eyes. Their moment didn't last long, however. The man that attempted to shoot her once before, pointed his gun at her again. Brooklyn saw it this time.

VLOOMP!

He fired.

BANG!
VLOOMP!

She appeared behind him, wrapped the chain around his neck, then flew almost thirty feet into the sky. The man had his hands on the chain around his throat.

His legs kicked wildly as he struggled to break free. Then, she saw Franklin. He locked eyes with her and shook his head. She was furious, but knew Franklin was right. She peered down at the man with disgust. *Killing someone isn't right. It isn't who I am, even if this man did just try to murder me.*

"You should count your blessings my mother taught *me* better than yours taught *you.*"

VLOOMP!

She transported the man to the warehouse miles away and dropped him to the floor. She removed the chain from his neck, rolled her eyes, then disappeared.

VLOOMP!

When the van made it to the surface, Dr. Classon drove off the lift and honked the horn. Tami slid the van door open.

"We need to go!"

VLOOMP!

Brooklyn appeared next to Franklin. A sly grin crept across her face.

"Race ya!"

"Go!"

VLOOMP!
ZIP!

They arrived simultaneously in the van, both seated next to each other, exhausted and relieved. It was a tie, though neither wanted to race again. They simply laughed.

CHAPTER 12
THE BOY

Franklin leaned over to slide the van door closed when he noticed another car approach and stop just outside of the gate. The passenger door opened, and a boy got out from the back seat. He was tall, but young, a teenager. He was slight of build, yet his muscles were well defined. He had light brown skin, the color of lightly stained wood, and a Mohawk with faded sides. He wore black jeans, black sneakers, and a tight black t-shirt that showed off his muscular arms covered in tattoos. He stared at Franklin. Franklin stared back.

The boy smiled, lowered his head, and then extended his arms out to his sides. Small cracking sounds could be heard as sparks started to fly on the metal gate, the gun turret, the generator on the roof and power lines above.

"Ummmm, I think we should go," Brooklyn suggested nervously.

"Great idea!" agreed Dr. Classon as he engaged the gears and began to pull off.

Franklin continued to watch the boy through the open door. The sparks grew bigger and louder. The arcs of electricity jumped from every metal surface and the overhead power lines. The sparks formed arches that hopped and danced and traveled to the boy. *Oh my God! HE is doing that!*

CRACKLE! BOOM! BOOM!

The streetlamps exploded in succession as electricity drained from them. The lights in the van began to flicker while the onboard computer screen dimmed and brightened.

Electrical energy wrapped around the boy's arms like large, electrical sleeves, growing bigger and bigger, louder, and louder. He clapped his hands together and screamed.

"UUUUUURRRRRRRRGHHHHAAAAAAHHHH!"

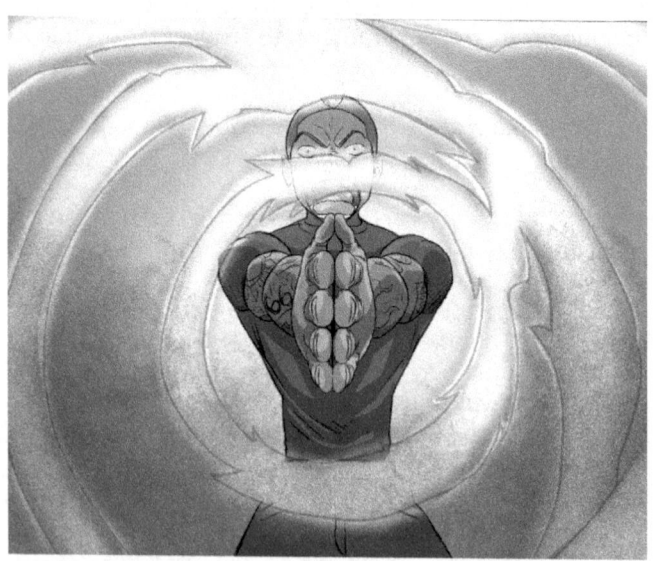

CRACK!

A bolt of pure electricity shot towards the van.

Dr. Classon, Tami and Brooklyn all screamed!

The bolt of electricity missed, though just barely. Franklin never screamed. He stood up, hung out of the van, and looked back at the boy as they drove away. They locked eyes from a distance. The boy flashed a devilish grin, then turned and got back into the car he arrived in. Franklin sat back down in the van and closed the door.

"WHO WAS THAT??" exclaimed Brooklyn.

"I don't know," a stunned Dr. Classon replied.

Franklin felt uneasy.

"We are going to see him again."

The siblings faced each other; the elation of their earlier triumph stolen from them by a frightening realization.

They weren't alone.

After a long drive, Dr. Classon, Tami, Franklin and Brooklyn found refuge in a small hotel, just off the service road. They didn't have an exact plan as to what to do next, they just knew they needed to get some rest. Dr. Classon and Tami combed over the data files she retrieved from the Company's off-site facility.

"Monroe, what is this?" exclaimed Tami.

Dr. Classon frowned as he studied one of the documents. It was a listing of test subjects that Dr. Classon assumed the Company had performed experiments on using the serum. What he read disturbed him.

January 17th, 2021

From: The Driver
To: The Director
Subj: Current Operatives

	AGE	M/F	STATUS	CODENAME
Subject #1	11	M	Deceased	"Vigor"
Subject #2	14	M	Operative	"Swarm"
Subject #3	13	F	Operative	"Recon"
Subject #4	11	F	Deceased	"Tonic"
Subject #5	9	M	Operative	"Bolt"
Subject #6	16	M	Operative	"The Boy"
Subject #7	17	F	Operative	"The Girl"
Subject #8	15	F	Deceased	"Portal"
Subject #9		**CLASSIFIED**		

Tami gasped as she read along with Dr. Classon.

"Are they experimenting on kids?"

"This was never supposed to happen," Dr. Classon answered regretfully. "But now, what I found earlier makes more sense."

"*What you found earlier?* What are you talking about?"

Dr. Classon quickly pulled up the lab results from Brooklyn's blood samples.

"You were there in the early stages of the serum, Tami. Remember when we first discovered the seven unique and unidentified genomes in the original sample?"

"Of course!" she replied. "It was unlike anything any of us had ever seen."

"Do you also remember when we discovered that older subjects tended not to survive?"

"Yes. There was a one in one thousand chance a subject would make it until Captain Santiago. He was the youngest subject to take the serum and survive."

Dr. Classon's head dropped.

"He still haunts me, Tami. Survive isn't the word I would use when it comes to him. What he has become... What we did to him, I.."

Tami put her arm around him to comfort him.

"We didn't know, Monroe. We thought we were helping him. But what does any of this have to do with this document?"

He sat up and began to type on the computer.

"Take a look at this," he responded as he pulled up the original sample.

Dr. Classon leaned over to see what Franklin and Brooklyn were up to. Brooklyn had just exited the bathroom after showering. Franklin sat on the edge of one of the two queen sized beds and angrily pressed buttons on the remote control to the television. Content that both were distracted, he leaned close to Tami and began to speak in a low, yet troubled tone.

"Brooklyn has six of those genomes."

"Her body accepted them that easily?" a surprised Tami inquired.

"Yes, if she was ever given the serum."

"She injected herself with Project Hover, Monroe. We watched her."

"True, but she presented the ability to teleport *prior* to that. This sample was taken before she injected herself. Both confirmed that at no time was she ever administered a serum before then. But that's not what's so troubling. Look at the genome sequence compared to the sequence of the original sample."

He clicked the button on the mouse and images of Brooklyn's genome sequence and one from the original blood sample were now side by side.

"Do you see it?" he asked Tami in an anxious whisper.

Tami leaned in. Her index finger danced from left to right as she swiped the screen between the images. She matched varying points between the two sequences, then her eyes grew wide.

"WAIT! THAT WOULD MEAN..."

"SHHHHHHH!" Dr. Classon scolded as he grabbed her thigh under the table.

Franklin heard the commotion. Dr. Classon poked his head from behind the screen and smiled.

"She's watching the True Spouses of New Jersey. She loves this show."

Franklin shook his head and turned back to search for something to watch.

"Crap TV!" he dismissively said.

Dr. Classon glared at Tami, his eyes wide.

"Sorry," she apologetically replied. "Monroe, if what I am seeing is true, then..."

"Then Brooklyn is related to the person that provided the original sample," Dr. Classon interjected to finish Tami's statement.

"But who?"

Dr. Classon clicked the mouse a second time. Brooklyn's sample was replaced by another. Tami became confused.

"Two images of the original sample?"

"No, it isn't."

He pointed to the sample on the left.

"This is the sample the Director provided us all those years ago."

He pointed to the sample on the right.

"This is the sample that I drew from Franklin a few hours ago."

"Impossible! Even if he was administered the purest form of the serum, there would be genetic differences between the two samples, with only the specific markers bonding to his strand as a mutation."

"Exactly. There are no mutations. No changes."

"If that's true, then..."

"Then the original sample came from Franklin. *He* is the source."

Dr. Classon sat back in his chair and leaned over to observe Franklin. Brooklyn now sat next to Franklin. She spoke to him about something, but Dr. Classon couldn't make out what. Tami turned to Dr. Classon.

"Monroe, how is it possible that a child from the future is here but his blood has been here for almost ten years?"

Dr. Classon never looked back at her. He continued to observe Franklin.

"I don't know, my love. But I don't think they are from the future."

Franklin continued to search for something to watch. He mashed the channel up button with great force. He didn't really care to find anything in particular. On the outside, he appeared frustrated. On the inside, he was scared and confused.

> *Who was that boy?*
> *How can he shoot lightning?*
> *How can he control electricity?*
> *How many more like him are out there?*
> *And why are they chasing us?*

"...and when you zipped over and hit him with that pipe?" Brooklyn recalled with great enthusiasm. "I was like..."

She noticed Franklin hadn't paid any attention to her. *He hasn't heard a word I've said!* She nudged him.

"Frankie.   Where are you?   You haven't said anything since we got here."

Franklin dropped his head in defeat. *How do I tell her I am scared? How do I tell her I don't know what we are gonna do?* He sighed.

"You're not scared?"

"Scared of what?" she asked.

He fearfully turned to her. "Scared of everything! Like, why are we here? Why is this happening to us?"

"Of course, I am!   But Frankie, we have superpowers! I mean like *for real, comic book, we need costumes superpowers!*"

"Yeah, but so did that kid. Brook, he shot lightning out of his arms! We can't beat that!"

"So that's what you're scared of. I ain't gonna lie; that freaked me out too. But you said you trusted Doc and he is like a mad scientist or something."

Franklin shifted his gaze and saw Dr. Classon leaning in his chair. Their eyes met. Brooklyn turned and watched Dr. Classon and Tami, then turned back to Franklin. Franklin's eyes were intense. Brooklyn's head tilted slightly to the left.

"You okay? Why are you staring at him like that?"
"I dunno, Brook. I am telling you; I have seen him before." His eyes then met hers. "I don't know where or when, but I know him, Brook."

187

Brooklyn turned around again to Dr. Classon. He had returned his focus to the computer.

"Do you still trust him?"

"For some odd reason, I do," he explained. "But there is something he isn't telling us. He knows more than what he is letting on."

Brooklyn's head swiveled. She gave Franklin a concerned stare.

"So, what are we going to do? You want to run? It's not like they could stop us."

"No. We are going to need them. I do want to find Uncle Jason, though."

"But it won't be our Uncle Jason. Wait, we know two different Uncle Jasons if we go off your version of events. Either way, neither of us would know him."

"True," Franklin agreed. "But I think an Uncle Jason is an Uncle Jason. He would be cool no matter where...or when we find him."

"Then its settled. Tomorrow we find..."

Suddenly, the television caught everyone's attention.

"We interrupt your regularly scheduled program for a special report."

"Good evening, I am Meredith Newton. Today, Channel Twelve Action News obtained exclusive footage that must be seen to be believed. In what police are referring to as a possible terrorist attack, two children seemed to have abilities that are normally reserved for the

pages of comic books or the silver screen. We warn you, some of the images you are about to see are graphic in nature. Viewer discretion is advised."

Dr. Classon and Tami leapt from the computer and joined Franklin and Brooklyn to watch. As the footage rolled, the four watched in anger. The news anchor narrated the footage and depicted Franklin and Brooklyn as villains. The news anchor stated *they* attacked the men in black and not the other way around.

"That's not what happened at all!" shouted Franklin angrily.

"They are making us seem like monsters! They came for us!!" Brooklyn said furiously.

Dr. Classon and Tami turned to each other. Franklin leaned forward and locked in on Dr. Classon.
"Are you seeing this, Doc?"

"Yeah, and where is the lightning thief that shot at us?" an angry Brooklyn added.

"This is the Company," Tami acknowledged.

"The Company?" asked Brooklyn.

"Yes. They have their clutches in everything. The media is no exception. They hacked into your security footage, Monroe," she replied.

Dr. Classon grew angry.

"And they scrubbed all footage of that boy."

This was the first time Franklin heard genuine concern in Dr. Classon's voice.

"You two should get some sleep," he instructed Franklin and Brooklyn. "We need to leave first thing in the morning."

"No! I want to see the rest of this first!" Franklin angrily replied.

"......twelve men were hospitalized, one is missing and presumed dead."

"The boy, pictured in this composite, seems to have the ability to move at incredible speeds. He is described as a black male, age thirteen to sixteen, standing approximately five-foot eight to five-foot ten, and weighing approximately one-hundred and sixty pounds. The internet has dubbed him The Veer, for his ability to move at unheard of speeds and change directions seemingly at will."

"The girl in the composite can apparently levitate. She is a black female, age thirteen to sixteen, standing approximately five-foot five to five-foot eight, and weighs approximately one-hundred and twenty pounds. The internet has dubbed her Gallow, an inexplicable nod to her soaring into the air and hanging the man now presumed dead."

If you have any information on the whereabouts of these dangerous criminals, please contact...."

Franklin turned the television off. He was angry, but something Brooklyn said moments earlier made him smile. *We do have powers!* The thought that people on the internet gave them nicknames excited him.

"The Veer. I kinda like that!"

"Gallow???" Brooklyn shouted, her faced scrunched up. "That's so morbid! And I didn't even kill him!"

"In any event," began Dr. Classon, "the news said you did. You're wanted now, which means people will be looking for us. Sleep, we have a long journey ahead of us."

"Where are we going, Monroe?"

"D.C."

"What's in D.C.?" asked Brooklyn.

Tami gave Dr. Classon a look of disapproval. She knew the moment he stated their destination who he wanted to find.

"Monroe, he will never help us."

"He has to," implored Dr. Classon. "He may be able to get us into the Company. By force if necessary."

He turned to Franklin and Brooklyn.

"If the world knows you exist, people will come after you, but just as many will see you as heroes. Superheroes, even. We're going to need help, and I know just the guy!"

Franklin turned to Brooklyn. "Superheroes?"

"Yeah," she shouted as her eyes lit up. "Superheroes!"

Franklin and Brooklyn smiled. They were superheroes now, and they liked it.

EPILOGUE
LATER THAT NIGHT...

The Director sat in her dark office; the only light emanated from the glow of the large screen that hung on the wall to the right of her desk. The twenty-foot by twenty-foot screen displayed footage of the events that unfolded at the chemical plant, taken from the Company's satellite in space. Though her desk was illuminated, her body remained in the shadows. Only her silhouette was visible, but barely. Her desk was made of glass and had a touchscreen computer embedded in it. She reached out and touched it. A terrified voice responded to the page.

"Yes, Ma'am?"

"Tell the board I won't be joining them today."

"Yes, Ma'am."

"And send in Courtland."

"As you wish, Ma'am."

She leaned back into her large, leather reclining chair. She rested her elbows on the armrests and folded her hands in front of her mouth. The office door swung open, and a nervous man shuffled over to her desk.

"Director. You asked to see..."

"How did Monroe Classon know they were here?" she asked disapprovingly.

"We ummmm...we believe he..."

"You *believe*?" she asked, her eyes left the screen that displayed the devastation Franklin and Brooklyn left in their escape.

"He...he traced their signature. The energy surge when they arrived caused a temporal spike at a very unusual location. We saw it but by the time our team arrived...he had...he had already made contact."

"Explain to me how a multi-billion-dollar conglomerate such as ours, with cutting-edge technology most world powers don't possess, was unable to recognize, what did you call it, a *temporal spike*? How did this multi-billion-dollar conglomerate with cutting-edge technology miss this temporal spike and *GET BEAT TO THE PUNCH BY A MAN WHO IS PLAYING SCIENTIST IN HIS BASEMENT*?!"

"We...ummmm...we..."

The man was in mortal fear for his life.

"*We* may need to find someone more...how shall I say this...*capable?*"

Then, she nodded. Dr. Courtland hadn't noticed the boy from the chemical plant had silently walked into the office and stood behind him. The boy touched Dr. Courtland's back with the tip of his finger.

ZAP!

A huge amount of electricity ripped through his back and across his heart. He died instantly. The stench of burned cloth and flesh became heavy.

"Find them, son. You have the full resources of the company at your disposal."

"Yes, Mother."

The Boy walked out of the office and closed the door behind him. The Director leaned back into her chair. Her ultimate goal was closer than she ever thought, and thanks to Franklin and Brooklyn's arrival, she now knew their location. She had long searched for the correct one, the universe in which they were hidden. She never expected they would appear in *this* one. But even with this knowledge, the Director felt dread.

They aren't alone. Monroe will have certainly tested them by now. He will learn the truth soon enough if he hasn't already. In every universe, Monroes are always meddlesome in that way, and the children's powers are awakening. I must inform the Grand Inquisitor.

The Director swiveled around in her chair and faced the wall behind her. She placed her hands out in front of her, palms up, and closed her eyes. A small ball of purple energy began to form and danced in her hands. She closed her eyes and focused her thoughts.

Grand Inquisitor. I must speak with you.

She waited patiently for a reply, her mind open. She listened for *his* thoughts. Then, a reply came as an echo in her mind.

Open the portal.

The Director spread her hands and moved them in a circular motion around the ball of energy. She drew her hands closer, collapsed the energy ball into a tight, small orb, then flung her hands out in front of her towards the wall. The orb expanded and stretched into a flat disc that hovered an inch off the wall. The energy disc measured ten feet in diameter and beamed bright light down onto the

Director's face. Gradually, a face began to take shape in the disc.

"What have you to report, Director Wayang?"

"Grand Inquisitor...we have a problem."

About the authors

Gamal Williams

Born in Brooklyn, NY, and having spent many of his formative years in Miami, FL, Gamal now resides in the Hampton Roads area of Virginia.

He joined the Navy in 1999 and became an Aviation Electronics Technician. He retired in 2019, after a successful twenty-year career at the rank of Senior Chief Petty Officer. He now spends his time writing and spending time with his children. A die-hard New York sports fan, music lover and avid reader, he ventured into writing as an outlet after a long battle with alcoholism. His first novel, "fin: a story of love and hope", started as a recurring dream he just could not shake. "JUMP" began in the middle of writing "fin."

"Gabe came to me one day and asked for a book. We were in the midst of the pandemic, and every bookstore was closed. We went online and found so few books that featured a little boy that looked like him as the lead character. So, I decided to write him one!"

  @authorgamalwilliams

www.authorgamalwilliams.com

(Background artwork by Amber Hightower. IG @theartofthevibe)

And introducing...

Gabriel Williams

Born in Portsmouth, Virginia, Gabriel is an energetic, imaginative, and intelligent 12-year-old young man, that loves drawing, and creating characters and new worlds. He came to his dad asking for a new book to read.

Unimpressed by the selection they found, Gamal began writing "JUMP" just for him. Soon, Gabriel joined in and helped develop the rich, fantasy world of JUMP.

Now, Gabriel and his dad write new adventures for Franklin, Brooklyn, and the rest of the JUMP family, and are hard at work on the next chapter in the JUMP series, "JUMP: Trial of Secrets."

"I like to draw and make up characters, and then I can't wait to tell my dad all about them."

 @authorgabrielwilliams

www.authorgamalwilliams.com

(Photo credit: Maria Jenkins IG: @riabphotography)

Cover and Illustrations by

Avoid Idle

 @avoididle